D1572512

ALL BUT SAFE

A PSYCHOLOGICAL SUSPENSE THRILLER

N. L. HINKENS

Text copyright @ 2023 Norma Hinkens

Published by Dunecadia Publishing, California

ISBN: 978-1-947890-46-6

Cover by: https://www.derangeddoctordesign.com/

Editing by: https://www.jeanette-morris.com/first-impressions-writing/

1

LEXI

I want what you have.

    My fingers shake as I pass the note to Cash—it's the second one to arrive this week, dropped off in our mailbox with my name scrawled across the envelope in red marker. The writing is childish looking, but the ominous tone is anything but.

The first note arrived three days ago, addressed to Cash: *Get rid of her, or I will.* It was a direct threat, but it made no sense—until now. The second note makes no bones about a motive. Someone wants my husband, and she wants him all to herself.

"It has to be someone you know, Cash," I say, pinching my bottom lip between my teeth as I search his face for an answer, any indication at all that he's taking this seriously.

He scratches the back of his neck, frowning, before shaking his head and tossing the note on the soapstone counter in the kitchen designed by his ex-wife, Anya. "I have no idea who it could be. It's messed up, that's for sure."

"Could it be someone who has a crush on you, at your office, perhaps? Does anyone give you weird vibes? Have you noticed anyone watching you, some reclusive wallflower who hangs on your every word?" I put a hand on my hip, skewering him with my gaze so he can't ignore me.

The crease between his brows deepens. "Everyone at work's pretty chill for the most part. Besides, wallflowers don't write notes threatening to get rid of people."

A shiver ripples down my spine. "You don't know that. Anyone can bluster when they're anonymous."

Cash pulls me close, wrapping a strong arm around my shoulders. "Hey, it's okay. I bet it's just a stupid prank—some socially awkward loser who's jealous of what we've got."

I look up at my handsome, six-foot-four husband and force a grin. "Let's hope you're right. Don't they say it's the quiet ones you have to watch?"

"Whoever *they* are." Cash winks and plants a kiss on my forehead. "Look, Lexi, we're not going to let this spoil the rest of our weekend, are we? What do you say we hop on the bikes and cruise around for a bit, find a new coffee shop to try?"

"O-kay," I say with a grin-and-bear-it sigh. I tuck the offending note next to the first one by the stack of mail on the counter. "I still think we should report this to the police. Even if it amounts to nothing, it's better to have a record of it, in case ... " My words trail off. I'm uncertain of what I'm trying to say. *In case it happens again? In case the situation worsens? In case this person turns out to be dangerous?*

Cash shrugs in his endearingly nonchalant manner. "Fine. I'll drop the notes off at the station on my way to work tomorrow."

I squeeze his hand gratefully. "Thanks. You're the best."

"Don't you know it!" he volleys back, striking an exaggerated Adonis pose.

I laugh, my eyes lingering on his smooth biceps, toned to

perfection courtesy of his rigorous gym schedule. Cash is not only easy on the eyes, he's the husband I've always wanted—a chocolate-hearted romantic, selfless, goal-oriented, and fun to be with. I knew he was perfect the first time I set eyes on him, and I had to have him. The bad part is that someone else shares my opinion of him—someone brazen enough to think they can take him away from me.

I won't let that happen.

2

CASH

Hot and sweaty after our bike ride, Lexi and I find our way to an eclectic coffee shop with mismatched furniture on a leafy street corner. "Why don't you grab that table outside and I'll get the drinks?" I say, motioning to a couple vacating a table in the shade.

I watch as Lexi weaves her way through the tables, her lithe frame deceptively slim for a woman in her second trimester.

I can't let her know how much the threatening notes concern me. I acted as though I had no idea who they're from, but I have my suspicions. Maybe I'm being overprotective because Lexi's pregnant, but I don't want to say anything to upset her or stress her out—anything that could harm our baby.

To say I was floored when I found out she was pregnant only five months into our relationship was an understatement. She broke down in tears when she told me, convinced I would break things off with her. Instead, I dropped to one knee and proposed—a spur-of-the-moment thing on my part. We hadn't known each other all that long, but I had just celebrated my thirty-fifth birthday, and I knew I wanted to settle down and have a family, a long-requested sibling for six-year-old Mila, my daughter with my ex, Anya. I couldn't wait to tell her the news—Mila that is, not my ex. Anya wasn't happy to hear about the baby because it means I'll be spending money on someone other than her and Mila. Money is all Anya seems to care about these days. She and I are civil to one another, but we're not close. Her affair gutted me. It's impossible for me to ever trust her again.

Drinks in hand, I make my way outside the coffee shop to join Lexi. "I was already in line when I realized I forgot to ask what you wanted. Will an iced hazelnut decaf latte work?"

"Perfect," she answers, reaching for the plastic cup and savoring a sip. She grins across at me mischievously. "It's your fault I'm hooked on these, you know."

I laugh and lean back in my chair, enjoying the light breeze on my face as I reflect on the day we met. Lexi was standing behind me in line at The Steamed Bean. I had just ordered an iced hazelnut latte, but when I reached for my wallet, I realized it wasn't in my back pocket where I normally keep it. "Sorry!" I said to the waiting cashier, after patting all my pockets in vain. "I must have left my wallet in my car. I'll have to dash back for it."

"No need," a woman's voice piped up behind me. She nodded to the cashier. "Go ahead and make it. I'll take care of his drink."

I tried to protest but she insisted. We ended up sitting together and talking for the best part of an hour, and then I asked her out to dinner that night. What had started out as a rough day, turned out to be fortuitous. I met my future wife and, as a bonus, an honest patron found my wallet lying in the gutter outside the coffee shop and turned it in.

Lexi and I were pretty much inseparable from then on. Everyone raised a collective eyebrow when I proposed five months later—no one more so than my overbearing mother.

"But you barely know the woman, Cash," she admonished me, her tattooed brows twitching indignantly. "Why the rush?"

"I'm ready to settle down, Mom. I want this baby as much as Lexi does."

"Yes, of course you do, but I'm worried this is only a rebound relationship. It's been less than a year since you and Jess broke up." She sighed in her usual dramatic fashion. "You two were so perfect together."

At the mention of Jess, my stomach had tightened, as it always does. Jess was the first and only girlfriend I had after my marriage broke up. We dated for a little over eighteen months—eighteen months and three days to be exact. We were shopping for engagement rings when she broke my heart out of the blue by telling me she'd decided to go back to school and get her PhD in computational mathematics, and that she wasn't ready to settle down and have kids for at least another few years. Stubbornly, I told her it was either me or the PhD. I walked away with my head held high and my heart in pieces. I truly loved her in a way I never loved Anya, and I still care about her, strictly as a friend, of course. At the end of the day, I only want the best for her. Jess is brilliant, and I could never stand in the way of her dreams—I just wish I could have been a part of them.

"I can't bear to see you get hurt again, Cash," my mother had rambled on. "You're a little naive when it comes to women—you have a knack for picking the fickle ones, and you've been through enough already in the last few years. Anya cheating on you, then Jess dumping you. I strongly suspect you're rushing into this marriage because you're afraid you're going to lose Lexi, too, if you don't propose."

"Maybe so, and if that's the case, I'm okay with it. I'm not going to back away from another chance at happiness just because I got burned before."

My mother stiffened her lips in a reproving manner but refrained from trying to dissuade me any further. After hemming and hawing about whether or not she could support my foolhardy decision, she showed up at our wedding, but it was painfully obvious she was there to convey her disapproval and not to celebrate our union.

"Cash? Are you even listening to me?" Lexi prompts, leaning across the checkered bistro table.

I blink and straighten up, reaching for my latte. "Sorry, I zoned out there for a minute. What was that last bit?"

She gives an incredulous shake of her head. "I was saying we should head home. We're going to your mother's for dinner tonight, remember?"

I swallow a large gulp of my lukewarm latte. It's been almost two months since the wedding and this is the first time my mother has invited us over to her house, even though she's been to our place for Sunday lunches, and dinner, several times. She's developed a habit of dropping by whenever she feels like it and inviting herself in. It must have finally dawned on her that she's going to have to accept Lexi as my wife if she wants to see her grandchild. Lexi's a trooper for even agreeing to go tonight. My mother makes no attempt to hide the fact that she dislikes her—distrusts her might be a better word. She told Lexi in no uncertain terms on our wedding day that she'd be out for blood if anyone dared to break her son's heart again.

Back at the house, we exchange a few words with our eighty-seven-year-old neighbor, Helen, who's ensconced in her rocker on the front porch, before stowing our bikes in the garage and making our way inside to shower and dress for dinner. I'm heading toward the stairs when the doorbell rings.

"I'll get it!" Lexi calls from the landing. "Lock the back door, will you?"

There's a muffled exchange in the entryway before she walks back into the kitchen, a dazed look on her face. "Cash, you ... have a visitor."

My breath catches in my throat when Jess steps into view, her effervescent air instantly filling the space. My fingers grip the edge of the kitchen counter like a vise. Unexpectedly seeing her here in my kitchen has left me momentarily disoriented.

"Hey, Cash!" she greets me, with a winning smile. "I wanted to pick up the iPad I left here. Thanks for the text. I'd forgotten all about it. Hope I didn't catch you at a bad time."

She slips the silky, lavender scarf I bought her for our first Christmas together from her neck and walks over for a hug. I wrap my arms stiffly around her, avoiding meeting Lexi's eyes.

"Actually, we're about to head over to my mother's for dinner," I say, releasing her. "The iPad's in my office. I'll ... grab it real quick." I flash Lexi a hollow smile as I exit the room, leaving her alone with Jess. My heart hammers in my chest as I stride down the hallway. I can tell from Lexi's expression she's far from happy at the unexpected visit. I can hardly blame her. She had no idea Jess and I were still in touch. I kept that small detail from her, simply because I didn't want to hurt her. In retrospect, I should have come clean. Now, it looks like I was trying to hide something nefarious, which I wasn't. I simply didn't want her to misunderstand our relationship. Jess was my best friend before she was my girlfriend, and that's not something easily erased.

I retrieve the iPad from the desk drawer in my office and hurry back to the kitchen, hoping I don't look as flustered as I feel. Lexi is gripping the back of a chair with both hands, knuckles drawn. Jess, on the other hand, is totally at ease, a congenial smile on her face.

"Here you go," I say, thrusting the iPad into her hands. "I came across it last week when I was cleaning out my office."

"Thanks." She slips it into her hand-stitched leather purse—the one we discovered together at the Creek Falls Arts and Crafts Fair. "It's just a backup anyway. I didn't miss it."

She turns to Lexi. "How far along are you now?"

"Fifteen weeks," she answers, barely managing to push the words through her lips.

Jess beams at her. "How exciting! I wish you all the best." She pulls her into an embrace that isn't reciprocated. "You look great. Pregnancy agrees with you."

Lexi simulates a tepid smile in response.

I walk Jess to the front door and wave her off, trying to quell a twinge of longing as I close the door on her intoxicating presence. My feelings for her are not a faucet I can switch on and off at will, despite my best intentions.

When I return to the kitchen, Lexi is seated at the table, staring into space.

"Are you okay?" I ask.

She shrugs. "She said you texted her. I didn't know you two were still in touch."

I wring my hands as though I can squeeze the guilt from

them. "Yeah, I'm sorry she dropped by without any warning. I forgot to tell you she might come by to pick up her iPad. She loaned it to me when mine broke, and I found it the other day when I was cleaning up."

"It's not that, it's just—" She shakes her head. "Forget it."

"Just what?" I take a step closer. "You can tell me. I get it if you're mad about her showing up at the house. Talk to me. I can see you're upset about something."

A perturbed look flickers across her face. "It's ... what she muttered in my ear when she hugged me goodbye. It gave me a bad feeling."

A knot of apprehension tightens in my stomach. Jess muttered something in my ear, too, as she was leaving, but I can't tell Lexi that. I clear my throat, trying not to sound overly concerned. "What did she say?"

Lexi locks a disconcerted gaze on me. "*Take care of him. You wouldn't want to lose him.*"

3

CASH

I spend almost the entire thirty-minute drive to my mother's house trying to convince Lexi that Jess didn't intend her words to come across as menacing.

"It sure sounded threatening to me!" she huffs, tucking her hands into her armpits. "Why would she say something like that?"

I'm dancing a fine line, trying to explain the complexities of my relationship with Jess without making it sound as if there's still something going on between us—which there isn't. I'm one-hundred percent committed to Lexi and our baby.

"*Take care of him* is a benign thing to say. It's kind of like Jess was passing the baton," I assure her, hoping it doesn't sound like I'm scratching around for an explanation. "It's just how Jess is. She's ... thoughtful."

"That's not how it came across to me," Lexi replies. "*You wouldn't want to lose him* sounded ominous."

"That's how you're choosing to interpret it. I'm sure she meant it in a sisterly kind of way—a piece of advice, if you like. She chose to prioritize her degree over our relationship, and she's had to live with the consequences of her decision. She simply wants us to be happy. She told me that."

Actually, the exact words she whispered to me when she was leaving were that she hoped Lexi and I would be *almost* as happy as she and I had been together—almost, but not quite. And then she'd laughed. Her eyes were dancing, but I don't think she was joking. Or maybe I just hoped she wasn't.

"Do you think Jess wrote those notes?" Lexi asks.

"What? No! Of course not," I splutter. "That's ridiculous."

I glance across at Lexi, alarmed to see tears clinging to her lashes. She's the sensitive sort, and hormones are likely playing havoc with her emotions. I remember Anya crying over every little thing when she was pregnant with Mila. I need to tread carefully, be a supportive spouse. But she's wrong to think Jess might be behind those nasty notes. "It's okay, babe," I say, softening my tone as I pull into the crushed gravel driveway outside my mother's house and switch off the engine. "I'm sorry if Jess was being inconsiderate. You won't have to see her again. So let's just forget all about her and focus on dinner."

Lexi grimaces. "And that's supposed to cheer me up? I've been dreading this dinner all day. I do my best to be pleasant, but your mother makes no attempt to hide her feelings about me—none of which are endearing."

"Don't worry. I won't let her gnaw on you all night. If she doesn't make an effort to be civil, we'll leave."

"Promise?" Lexi sniffles, wiping her eyes with the back of her hand.

"I promise," I say, bringing my lips to hers.

After a moment or two, Lexi pulls away and nudges me.

"Um, your mother's standing on the front steps glaring at us like we're illegally parked in her driveway."

I blow out a breath as I reach for the door handle. "That's our summons to dinner."

"Lexi," my mother says, with a stiff nod of her sprayed curls by way of greeting when we reach the front steps. "Not exactly blooming, are we? You look rather haggard. Just wait until the baby comes." She tinkles a laugh. "Now *that's* exhausting!"

I almost say something I'll regret, but I manage to bite my tongue. We can't turn around and leave without at least giving this a chance. I need to pick my battles, and I have no doubt we'll have at least one run-in over the course of the evening. At least Mom's not ignoring my wife like she did at our wedding.

Her eyes settle on Lexi's inconspicuous belly. "Are you sure you're eating healthily, my dear? I would hate to think you're stunting my grandchild's growth at this critical stage."

Lexi gives a pinched smile. "Thanks for your concern, Eleanor. Rest assured, our baby's getting all the nutrition they need."

My mother raises a skeptical brow before leading the way into the dining room.

"I brought you our latest sonogram picture," Lexi says, striking an optimistic beat as she fishes it from her purse. "My doctor says the baby's growth is right on target and the heartbeat is strong."

Mom holds the photo up close to her face and squints at it. "I can't tell if it's a boy or a girl. Aren't you supposed to be able to tell by now?"

"We want to keep it a surprise," I say, winking at Lexi.

My mother tuts her disapproval. "Why on earth would you refuse to find out the child's sex in this day and age?

Hopelessly impractical! Cash, darling, why don't you pour us some wine while I fetch the chicken casserole. Lexi, set that picture in my office and then join me in the kitchen."

I shoot Lexi an apologetic look. She doesn't like my mother's chicken casserole—which might be why Mom made it. She dropped one off after we came back from our honeymoon and then sat in our kitchen watching like a sadistic prison guard as Lexi forced down a few mouthfuls. I open a bottle of cabernet and pour two glasses, then fill Lexi's glass with water. She could probably use a swig of wine to wash down the casserole, but I'm sure my mother has Child Protective Services on speed dial for such an eventuality.

"Here we are!" she announces as she makes her triumphant entrance, holding aloft a blue stoneware serving dish. "My famous chicken casserole! I made it especially for you, Lexi, taking into consideration the fact that you can't have anything too spicy."

Lexi's smile freeze dries to her face. "Thanks," she mutters, as my mother piles a heaped serving on her plate.

I squeeze Lexi's knee gently under the table as she picks up her fork with a determined air.

"Have you given any thought to childcare after the baby is born?" my mother enquires. "Not that I'm volunteering. I'm far too busy with all my charities."

"I'll have eight weeks maternity leave," Lexi answers. "I'm thinking about returning to work part-time after that. It's only a five-minute drive from our house. Cash and I can work around each other's schedules."

My mother stabs at a piece of chicken like she's making sure it's dead. "You can't expect Cash to adjust his work schedule to suit your whims. He has an important job with contractual obligations. He's working his way up the proverbial engineering ladder. It's not a dead-end retail job like yours, dear. You can't expect him to take time off to change diapers so you can earn minimum wage folding sweaters and restocking shelves in a department store." She sighs dramatically. "And to think Jess is working on her PhD now. She and Cash were such a power couple."

"Mom!" I set down my fork and glare across the table at her. "Lexi's a floor manager. It's hardly a dead-end job. Do you have to be so rude and condescending?"

She widens her eyes in mock innocence. "Cash, darling. It's simply a turn of phrase. The point I'm trying to make is that you're the main breadwinner and Lexi shouldn't do anything to jeopardize that, especially now you're going to have two children to support." She inserts a dramatic pause. "And two wives."

"Anya's my ex-wife," I correct her. "I don't pay alimony anymore."

My mother flutters her fingers dismissively. "Current, ex, whatever. The fact is, you're still supporting Anya's child."

"We should get going," Lexi interrupts, pinning a pleading gaze on me. "It's been a long day. I'm exhausted after our bike ride."

"*Bike* ride," my mother echoes in a tone of mock horror. "That's reckless, riding a bike when you're pregnant, risking injury to the baby—"

"Mom! Please! We're more than capable of assessing the risk ourselves. Thanks for dinner, but we really need to head home now. We have work tomorrow and Lexi needs her rest."

"But you haven't had dessert, yet. I made your favorite— lemon meringue pie."

"Great," I say getting to my feet. "We'll take it to go."

· · ·

Safely back in the car, I plug in my seatbelt and turn to Lexi. "You're a rockstar. I know that wasn't easy."

She shakes her head forlornly. "I don't understand why she dislikes me so much. Why would she go out of her way to make her chicken casserole when she knows I don't like it. It's as though she delights in tormenting me."

I squeeze the bridge of my nose, selecting my words with care. "I don't know. Maybe it slipped her mind, and she was just trying to think of something mild to cook that wouldn't upset the baby." I keep my eyes forward as I start the engine. I'm sure it was deliberate, but I hate to see Lexi hurt, and I'm desperate to believe the lie myself.

Lexi throws me a skeptical look. "Is that why she made lemon meringue pie for dessert when she knows perfectly well you're not supposed to eat it when you're pregnant?"

I elevate my brows a fraction. "You're not?"

Lexi sighs. "The egg whites in the meringue aren't cooked all the way through. I'm sure she knows that, even if you're clueless."

I pull out of the cul-de-sac, not wanting to argue the point. I don't like to think of my mother being malicious. Catty, yes. Condescending, definitely—but not bent toward evil. Surely, she wasn't deliberately trying to make my wife ill. She might not be aware that lemon meringue pie is on the banned foods list for pregnancy. Or she could have forgotten. After all, it's been thirty-five years since she had me. Sometimes I feel like I'm stuck between a rock and a hard place when it comes to keeping the women in my life happy. Deep down, I know they both want the best for me. My mother has always been difficult, but she's all I have, and I can understand why she's having a hard time warming up to a new daughter-in-law. It was all so sudden—my proposal after a mere five months of dating, a hurriedly thrown together wedding, and the baby, of course.

My mother told me outright that she's suspicious of Lexi's intentions after being *fooled* as she put it by Anya and Jess. She asked if I thought Lexi had intentionally got pregnant to trap me—which I don't believe for a minute. The truth is, I don't have a good track record when it comes to relationships, and my mother's afraid Lexi will leave once the baby is born, tying me to yet more alimony and child support. But she's not being fair to Lexi—she just needs to give her a chance. Lexi's nothing like Anya. She would never cheat on me, and she'll never walk out on me. I'll do everything in my power to make sure of it.

Twenty minutes later, I pull into our garage and reach into the back seat for my coat. As I climb out of the car, Lexi lets out a horrified gasp.

"What's wrong—" My voice trails off when I see the message spray-painted on the side of our house.

4

LEXI

I stand next to the car, glued to the asphalt, shoulders shaking as I take in the noxious red paint weeping down the side of our house.

You don't deserve a baby.

"Come on, let's get you inside," Cash says, wrapping a protective arm over my shoulders and whisking me through the front door. He walks me to the kitchen where I sink gratefully into a chair.

"Who would do something like that?" I rasp, hugging my shivering frame. "Do you think it's the same person who sent the notes?"

Cash sweeps a hand over his brow as he considers the possibility. "I don't know, but I'll make it my business to find out. First, I'm going to make you a cup of tea, and then I'll take care of the paint. It's fresh so it should come off easily enough."

I grab his sleeve before he can move away. "It must have been someone who knew we were gone this evening."

Cash frowns. "Not necessarily. It could have been a random drive by."

I give an adamant shake of my head. "This wasn't random. Only two people knew we were going to your mother's this evening: Helen—who's hardly up to the task of defacing our property—and Jess."

The expression on Cash's face darkens. "What are you suggesting—that Jess did this?"

I give a helpless shrug. "I don't know. What else am I supposed to think? Helen can scarcely manage more than a few steps on her walker. Besides, she has no reason to do something like that." I rub my fingers across my brow. "Although, I suppose she could have told Wade we were going out."

The trench on Cash's brow deepens. We love our sweet, elderly neighbor, Helen, but neither of us hold any affection for her adult, pothead son who lives in her detached, converted garage behind the main house.

"I wouldn't put it past Wade to do something like this," I go on. "When Helen gave me a pair of booties she crocheted for the baby last week, Wade snarled something about how he wasn't going to stand for a wailing baby next door."

"I suppose he could have done it in a fit of rage," Cash says, a preoccupied look on his face. "He did throw that trash over our fence when I asked him to clean it up last week."

I nod glumly. "Exactly! He has it in for us. We can't ignore this. We have to confront him—file charges. It's vandalism."

"But we don't know for sure if it was him."

"What's the alternative?" I stare at Cash, waiting on him to draw his own conclusions.

He swallows hard as he considers the implications of what I'm saying. He doesn't want to believe Jess is capable of doing anything like this, but he underestimates her. Jess is clever, and clever people can be manipulative. I know she and Cash had a strong bond, and even though he's assured me he's over her, I'm not convinced of it. He told me he broke things off when she decided to postpone starting a family and get her PhD instead. But Eleanor told me he regretted it afterward and tried everything to get back with her. The problem is, I can't trust Eleanor to tell me the truth either. She's good at planting seeds of doubt. It's not only me she gets her tentacles into—she feeds Cash shady remarks and insinuations about me leaving him high and dry once the baby's born. Nothing could be further from the truth. I will never leave him.

"Maybe we shouldn't clean the paint off until we've talked to the police," I say. "Someone is targeting us, whoever it is—none of this is random. They're making it clear they're not happy about us being together." I move my hand protectively over my belly. "This has to end before the baby comes. I don't want to live with this hanging over my head."

Cash kneels in front of me and takes both my hands in his. "You won't have to. I'll sort this out, I promise. I'll take a photo of the message on the wall and show it to the police on Monday, along with the notes. If nothing else, at least we'll have documented the harassment."

"The other thing that makes me think it wasn't random," I say, furrowing my brow, "is that there's no exterior camera on the east side of the house. Whoever graffitied that wall must have known that."

Cash nods. "I'll install a couple of extra cameras. No one will be able to get close again without being spotted."

"Will you have time to do it before you leave for Vegas on Friday?"

Cash slams a palm to his forehead. "I totally forgot the

bachelor party was this weekend. Don't worry, I'll make time. I'm not leaving you alone unless you feel safe in your own house." He stands and pulls me to my feet. "Come on, time for bed. You need your rest, and we both need to be up early."

I head into the bathroom to brush my teeth while Cash looks for a clean shirt for the morning. When I'm done, I walk barefoot into the bedroom and make my way over to the walk-in closet. Cash grimaces and pulls the door closed behind him, his face drained of color. "Don't go in there."

I give an uncertain laugh. "I need to pick out an outfit for work tomorrow."

He shakes his head slowly. "Not right now."

"Why? What's going on?"

"Nothing. I just need to ... clean up in there, that's all."

"What's that smell?" I ask, wrinkling my nose.

Cash hardens his jaw, a stricken look on his face.

I elbow my way past him and shove the closet door wide open, the overpowering odor of bleach filling my nostrils.

5
_____

LEXI

My maternity clothes are ruined. Every last stitch. They're not just splattered with bleach —it looks like someone dunked them in the stuff and hung them up to drip dry onto the hardwood floor below. A slow, methodical drip eating through both my floor and my dreams like acid.

I stumble backward, one hand pressed to my mouth. "Call 911! Now!"

Cash is already pulling out his phone. "Okay, calm down. I'll call the station. This isn't an emergency situation."

"How do you know that?" I drop my voice, peeking nervously over my shoulder. "What if someone's still in the house?"

Cash's eyes dart to the hall, as he dials the number. "I'll take a look around in a minute to make sure the coast is clear."

I listen as he relays the incident to an officer who promises to send someone out to the house right away.

I follow close behind Cash as he makes the rounds and checks the other bedrooms. Nothing else appears to be disturbed. This was a targeted attack with a clear message. Someone does not want me to have Cash's baby. And I know who that person is. The problem is going to be convincing Cash.

"How did they get into the house?" I ask as we head downstairs to wait for the police. "The front door was locked, and there's no sign of a break-in."

Cash marches across the kitchen and twists the knob on the back door. He turns to me with a look of dismay. "This door's unlocked."

I gape at him. "Are you serious? I told you to lock it before we left."

"I did." He squeezes the bridge of his nose. "At least, I think I did. When Jess showed up out of the blue, it threw me off. Maybe I forgot. No! I remember now. I definitely locked it before we took off for Mom's."

"You *thought* you did, but evidently you didn't," I retort, my voice breaking. "My maternity clothes are ruined, and I haven't even had a chance to wear most of them, yet."

"I'm sorry Je—*Lexi*. I'm sorry, Lexi." He rubs his hands frantically over his face. "I don't know why that came out just now. My mind's a mess."

I shake my head in disgust, salty tears trickling down to the corners of my mouth. "She's always front and center in your mind. You're worried she might be behind this, and you don't want to admit it. She wants you back! Can't you see that? She wants me out of the way!"

"Lexi, please!" Cash takes a step toward me, but I hold my palms out in front of me. "Don't touch me!"

"Look, if I thought for a minute Jess had anything to do with this, I'd drive to her apartment right now and have it out with her. But that's not who she is. She would never do something as sick as this."

"Then who else would? It's personal. This is our baby they're targeting!"

Cash wets his lips. "I don't know—Wade, maybe? You said he made that weird comment about not wanting a wailing baby next door. He's a pothead and an alcoholic. Maybe he has a record for all we know. I'll tell the police what he said to you. If he's behind this, they'll get to the bottom of it."

OFFICER PRICE, who shows up to take the report, is a dumpy man with a graying mustache and a bad habit of clearing his throat too loud and too often. A faint smell of cigarette smoke clings to his clothes. I wouldn't have pegged him as a smoker, but apparently, he has more than one vice. From the outset, he appears dismissive, barely glancing at the sickening message daubed on the exterior wall. I take an instant dislike to him, but I do my best to mask my feelings. We need him on our side.

"It has all the markings of a personal attack," he agrees, after listening to everything Cash tells him, and taking the notes into evidence. "Any idea who might be behind this? Do you have any enemies?"

I try to repress a shudder at his heavy-lidded blink, picturing a foot-long tongue shooting out through his shriveled lips.

"We did wonder about our next-door neighbor's adult son," Cash replies. "He's a bit of an oddball—a pothead— and he made a rude comment about not wanting to put up with a crying baby when he heard my wife was pregnant."

Price jots down the information. "I'll have a word with him after we're done here. Anyone else in your circle of acquaintances who's not happy about the pregnancy?" He looks up, directing the question at me.

I grit my teeth, trying to keep my expression neutral. *Only my husband's ex-wife, his ex-girlfriend, and his mother.* If Cash weren't here, I might actually say that out loud. But he would never forgive me for throwing the other women in his life under the bus. The last thing I need is for him to feel the need to defend them and make me look like the insecure, new wife.

What he should be wondering is if they're collaborating to make my life miserable—the enemy of your enemy is your friend, after all.

6
———

CASH

I haven't told Lexi about the gift that was delivered to my office this morning—a stunning black Montblanc pen engraved with my name in gold lettering. I looked it up online and I'm reeling with shock at the price of it, but even more so at the message in the card that accompanied it: *Write me back into your future.*

I've gone around and around in my head trying to decipher it. Is Lexi right that Jess secretly wants me back? But why would she not just tell me to my face? She's had ample opportunity, and she's nothing if not forthright. Why launch a vindictive campaign directed against my wife, even going so far as to destroy her maternity clothes? It's not as if Lexi's the reason Jess and I broke up—she wasn't even on the scene back then. Is it because of the baby? Is that what has triggered this?

I lean back in my office chair and plunge my hands through my hair as if that will somehow magically untangle the mess I'm in. I know one thing for sure. I can't tell Lexi about the latest message and the extravagant gift that accompanied it. It will only confirm her worst fears that Jess is behind everything—which seems increasingly likely despite my protests to the contrary. The pen is a dead give-away—a sign of sorts. Jess and I always exchanged meaningful gifts with each other, although never anything this expensive.

The truth is, I don't know whether to be flattered or angry, or where to go from here. There's no way I can accept the gift. It would be a betrayal of my marriage. Lexi doesn't deserve to be hurt like this, especially not now when she's carrying our child. I'm plagued with guilt about the whole situation because, deep down, the idea that Jess has come to regret her decision, and wants us to get back together, sends a shard of excitement through me.

I push the thought to the back of my mind. It can never happen—absolutely not. That ship has sailed. I'm committed to Lexi and our unborn child, and I won't do anything to jeopardize my chance at a stable family.

After giving it some thought, I decide to stash the gift in the bottom drawer in my desk until I can figure out what to do with it. I can't in good conscience simply throw away a pen worth close to five-hundred dollars. If it did come from Jess—and what other option is there, if I'm being honest—I have to return it to her. I could mail it back, but I'd rather meet with her face-to-face and make it clear that this can't continue—the gifts, the notes, the petty vandalism.

I suppose there's a possibility the notes and the vandalism aren't connected. There's still a chance Wade might have defaced my house in a fit of rage over the trash incident, but I doubt he could identify my wife's maternity attire. That part doesn't add up.

By the end of the day, I've made up my mind to confront Jess and get it over with. I don't want this uncertainty hanging over my head when I'm in Vegas this weekend. And

I definitely don't want Lexi worrying that something else might happen while I'm gone. I pull out my phone and type a quick message to Jess.

I got the gift. I can't accept it.

Her reply is almost instantaneous. *What gift???*

I clench my jaw as I stare at the screen. So this is how it's going to be. Irritated, I tap out a response.

We need to talk. Meet me in 30 at our usual spot?

See you there!!!

I pocket my phone and head out to my car, heart fluttering in my chest. Jess sounded eager to meet with me—too eager. Almost as though she was waiting for me to ask. I'm not sure what game she's playing, but it's a dangerous one. Someone's going to end up getting hurt. I wish I could trust myself to make sure it's not Lexi. I start the car, then send her a quick text telling her I'm going for a drink with my boss before heading home. It doesn't make me feel good to lie to her, but at least it won't raise any red flags. Grabbing a drink with colleagues after work is something I do on a regular basis to hammer out details of projects we're working on.

I arrive at the pub first and find a quiet booth at the back. A waitress comes by, and I order two pints of Jess's favorite beer. I still remember everything about her, from her favorite song—*Stairway to Heaven*—to her favorite beach in the world—*Smugglers Cove on the coast of Zakynthos in Greece*. That's where I told her I couldn't imagine life without her, and she told me I didn't have to because she felt the same way.

"I'm impressed you remembered my favorite draft."

I startle, spilling a few drops of my beer, when Jess slides into the green padded seat opposite me, grinning her electric smile. "Yikes, Cash. You look like you've just been fired. Rough day at the office?"

She, on the other hand, looks good, glowing in fact. I momentarily lose my train of thought, imagining her pregnant with my child instead of Lexi. I wonder if the baby would look like her—I certainly hope so. Disgusted at myself, I shake my head loose of the thought, and try to refocus on why I'm here. I slip my hand into my coat pocket, pausing briefly to allow the waitress to set down our drinks, before placing the luxurious, black pen box on the table.

"What's this?" Jess asks, flipping open the lid without waiting for an answer. She lets out an admiring whistle. "That's gorgeous. What did you do, get a promotion or something? Is that what we're celebrating?"

I take a hasty sip of my beer and brush the back of my hand over my lips. "Don't play games with me, Jess."

I dig out the card and set it next to the pen. "*Write me back into your future*—seriously? Why now? You know Lexi's pregnant. Believe me, I wish it could have been different, too, but I'm a married man now, in case you've forgotten. You didn't want any part of family life, remember?"

Jess raises her eyebrows a fraction. "Cash, this isn't from me. You didn't think—" She leans across the table gazing into my eyes with a hint of amusement on her lips. "It's not that I didn't *want* you, per se, it's just that we wanted other things, and the timing wasn't right. I thought we'd worked all this out already."

I shrug. "I thought so too, until this landed on my desk this morning. And there were other messages, delivered to the house."

Jess sips her beer. "Sounds cryptic. Are you going to enlighten me?"

I hesitate, suddenly unsure of myself. I was almost

certain the gift was from her. Who else would drop that kind of money on me? Admittedly, it's a stretch to think she's behind the vandalism. Have I got this all wrong?

"Cash?" she prompts.

"Someone spray painted a nasty message on the side of our house," I blurt out.

"What kind of message?"

I let out a long, shuddering sigh. "You don't deserve a baby."

Jess's eyes widen. "That's twisted! Did you call the police?"

I give a vacant nod, suddenly eager to unload all my fears on someone who understands me better than anyone else. "It gets worse. I accidentally left the back door unlocked when we went out last night and someone came into the house. They threw bleach all over Lexi's maternity clothes—they're destroyed."

Jess's mouth drops open. "What a sick thing to do! Lexi must be terrified."

"She is," I agree, staring at the amber liquid in my glass. "We both are. I've ordered more exterior cameras to make sure it can't happen again."

"That's good." She gives an approving nod. "Lexi needs to feel safe when you're not there. I know she won't get much support from your mother."

I give a hesitant smile as I take a swig of my beer. Typical Jess to be concerned about Lexi's welfare. How could I have suspected her of being behind any of this? But if it wasn't her, who was it?

Jess reaches across the table and slides her hand over mine. An electric jolt goes through me at her touch. My insides are melting more rapidly than an ice cream cone in a heatwave. I struggle to refrain from pulling her into my arms.

"None of this was my doing. You know that, don't you?" she says.

"Yes. Of course. It's just that when I saw the card, I thought ... I don't know." What I want to say is that I was secretly hoping the card was from her, and that she's ready to admit that she wants me back. But I clamp my lips shut before the truth slips out and betrays me as the faltering husband I am.

"Do you have any idea who could be behind it?" Jess goes on, her gaze burrowing so deep into my soul it hurts.

"None whatsoever."

"Someone you dated years ago, perhaps?"

I let out a snort. "I can't think of anyone who kicked me to the curb in high school and wants me back now. Anya's still happily married to Anton, with his bottomless trust fund, and why wouldn't she be? They're currently touring around Europe for six weeks. You're pursuing your PhD like you always wanted to—like you should." I give a self-conscious chuckle. "I'm just not that popular."

Jess knits her brows together. "In that case, maybe it's someone from Lexi's past trying to sabotage her by posing as your ex."

7

CASH

I twist my glass between my fingers, weighing Jess's theory against what little I know about Lexi's past. She told me her last serious relationship ended two years before we met, when her boyfriend at the time dumped her and moved to Australia. That pretty much rules him out, and she's never mentioned anyone else from her past who might be holding a grudge. Then again, it's not as if I'd know if she was lying to me. We were still in the getting-to-know-all-about-each-other phase when she accepted my impulsive proposal.

"I should get going," I say, after glancing at my watch. "Lexi's expecting me home for dinner."

Jess drains her glass and raises it in a toast. "Cheers! To exes who can still be friends. I'm sorry you're going through this, Cash. It sucks. I was so happy for you when I heard you were going to be a father again. I know it's what you've always wanted. Keep your chin up. I'm sure this person will soon get bored with their amateur stunts and move on. Either that or the police will put an end to their antics."

"Let's hope you're right. I'm off to Vegas this weekend for

Tom's bachelor party, and I hate the thought of leaving Lexi alone knowing some creep is trying to terrify her."

Jess pulls her hair back over her shoulders with a practiced flick of her thumbs—a gesture I always found particularly endearing. Is there anything about her I didn't find endearing?

"If I can help, just say the word. I'm here for you, always —you know that." She hesitates and then adds, "If you want, I can go by the house and check on Lexi while you're gone."

I try to keep my expression neutral as I picture the look of horror on Lexi's face if I dared suggest such a thing. "Thanks, Jess. I appreciate that. I'll let you know if I need anything." I give her a quick peck on the cheek before hurrying out to my car. Despite my best intentions, her tantalizing scent lingers in my nostrils, driving me to distraction on the way home.

LEXI HAS chicken piccata waiting for me when I walk into the house. I sweep her into a guilty hug and kiss her. "Did I ever tell you you're the best?"

She laughs. "All the time. That was a long day. How was work?"

"It was all right. Did those cameras arrive?"

She gestures to two packages on the counter as she serves up the food. "Let's eat first, then you can dive into that project."

"Any drama at the store today?" I ask when we sit down at the table.

She reaches for the pepper shaker and douses her chicken with it. "It was boring, slow, unremarkable—exactly how you'd expect a day in a dead-end job to go."

I grimace at the dig, but she wiggles her brows at me to let me know she's kidding.

"I'm sorry about how Mom behaved last night," I say. "I gave her the benefit of the doubt thinking she might have been trying to make amends by having us over. I should have known better."

Lexi spears a piece of broccoli and waves it in front of her. "I don't get why she loathes me so much. I've done everything I can to make her feel special as the grandmother of our child. It's as if she wants to sabotage me or something."

I glance up, my fork frozen halfway to my mouth. *Sabotage.* Jess used that word, too. Is that what this is about? A campaign of sabotage? Could my own mother possibly be involved? She does have a mean-spirited streak. Anya and Jess have both felt her wrath in the past—exacerbated after they ended their relationship with me in what my mother perceived to be nothing short of treason. But Lexi hasn't done anything deserving of her vile treatment.

"What is it?" Lexi asks, arching a brow.

"Nothing. I just feel bad about what happened. I won't ask you to go over to Mom's again. Not until she straightens up. It's going to take time for her to warm up to you. She doesn't want to see me hurt again."

"That's fair. I just wish she'd give me a chance."

"She will once the baby's born—you'll see." Truthfully, I'm beginning to have my doubts, but that's the last thing Lexi needs to hear right now.

After we've finished clearing away the dinner dishes, I grab some scissors and reach for the parcels on the counter. The larger box contains the new cameras I ordered from Amazon. I glance through the installation instructions and then turn my attention to the smaller package. After slitting it open, I pull out the contents, frowning in confusion as I hold up a navy T-shirt and read the lettering on the front: *Never gonna say goodbye.*

"Why did you order that?" Lexi asks, peering over my shoulder.

"I ... uh, I didn't."

"What do you mean?" She snatches up the packing slip, scowling as she reads aloud: "Think of me when you wear this. Miss you babe! xoxo."

Her face tightens. "This is from Jess, isn't it?"

I toss it onto the table. "No, it's not!"

"How do you know that?"

"I just do."

Lexi narrows her eyes, her piercing gaze never leaving my face. "What's going on between you two, Cash? Why didn't you tell me you were still in contact with her?"

"I'm not. I told you already. I found her iPad when I was clearing out my office. I texted her to see if she wanted it back, that's all." I avert my eyes as I reach for the cameras.

That's not all, but that's all she needs to know. Telling Lexi the truth would kill her. I'm beginning to fear that's someone's end game.

8

CASH

When I land in Vegas, my phone pings with a message from an unknown number: *We belong together. You can't lose me.*

A second ping. *Are you wearing your T-shirt?*

The hairs on the back of my neck begin to tingle. Not again. This is the fifth message I've got this week, all variations of the same theme, all from different numbers—presumably, prepaid phones. If it isn't Jess, who keeps sending these texts? Surely not my own mother. I can't imagine she even knows what a prepaid phone is, let alone how to use one to cover your tracks. Then again, the internet is an equal opportunities teacher.

"Turn that thing off, man," Tom says, reaching into the overhead bin for his bag. "Time to disconnect. We're here to party."

I give a forced laugh. "Yeah, try telling that to my pregnant wife."

Tom pulls a face. "So that's what I've got to look forward to."

I clap him on the back and grin. "Commiserations, man."

IT'S ALMOST two in the morning before I stagger back to my room in the Mandalay Bay Hotel and throw myself across the bed. I'm hammered, but I pull out my phone and check it for messages, nonetheless. I've had it on airplane mode all evening, partly to appease Tom, and partly for my own sanity. I talked to Lexi earlier and let her know we'd be out late, so she isn't expecting me to call again until tomorrow. She assured me she's fine, and promised to make sure all the doors and windows were locked before she went to bed. The new cameras are installed and operational, which gives me some peace of mind.

I blink blearily at my phone screen trying to scan the multiple messages popping up in quick succession. My stomach churns. What now? Is there no end to the harassment? Groaning, I sit up and turn on the reading lamp at the side of the bed. Along with several texts, I'm surprised to see two missed calls from my mother. I open up the message thread, expecting to be summoned to the house to reconnect her Wi-Fi or some other such equally trivial technological issue she can't wrap her head around.

Instead, I'm bombarded with a slew of panicked messages: *Call me as soon as you get this ... Lexi's at the hospital ... No updates, yet ...*

My brain sputters to life as I fumble with my phone and dial my mom's number. I rake my hands through my hair trying to gather my senses as I wait for her to answer. It's far too early for the baby to come. I can't believe this is happening—this weekend of all times. It must be the stress of everything Lexi's been through. I shouldn't have left her alone after what happened. What was I thinking? Someone threatened to get rid of her, and I installed a couple of extra cameras and left her to fend for herself. I should have cancelled this weekend. Tom would have understood. I'm a lousy husband. Stupid. Senseless. Selfish—

"Cash! Finally!" my mother exclaims. "Why didn't you answer my—"

"Is Lexi all right?" I rasp. "Is it the baby?"

"She's going to be fine, the baby's fine. I drove to the wrong hospital—she got confused and thought she was at College Hospital on Pacific Avenue. It was College on Ninth and Fairhaven. Anyway, she's back home now—she just needed a few stitches, as it turns out."

I sink back on the bed, weak with relief. *Stitches!* "What happened? Did she fall?"

My mother lets a dramatic pause unfold before responding. "She very foolishly went for a walk alone in the park this evening and some drugged-up homeless person came at her with a knife. Fortunately, he barely grazed her forearm —five stitches in total. She drove herself to the ER and she's back home now. I hope I didn't scare you, darling. I thought it was much worse when she called me. You'd think a grown woman would have known better than to go walking by herself in an isolated section of the park. Foolhardy, if you ask me—endangering the life of your child like that. I told her as much over the phone."

I squeeze my eyes shut, picturing Lexi cringing under my mother's tirade. "Why didn't she call me?"

"She said your phone was turned off."

"I'll call her right now."

"It's the middle of the night, son. Best let her sleep. And you should get some sleep too—you sound dreadful. I hope you're not drunk."

Before she can launch into a lecture, I hang up and send Lexi a text: *Just talked to Mom. I'm so sorry, babe. Call me any time. I can catch an early flight home. Love you lots. xoxo.*

When she doesn't respond, I plug my phone into the charger and place it on the bedside cabinet. I was exhausted when I stumbled into my room, but I'm wide awake now. My mind is all over the place, the alcohol only stringing my incoherent thoughts into ever more frightening scenarios. Things have taken a sinister turn. I don't believe it was a coincidence that Lexi was attacked in the park. Is it connected to everything else that's been happening? Did someone know I was out of town? Do they know her schedule?—Lexi goes for a walk in the park most evenings around the same time. Or maybe whoever is behind all this followed her there. Someone from Lexi's past? A man, apparently—not Jess, and not my mother. It was crazy of me to think either of them could have been involved. Mom was obviously upset about Lexi being attacked—worried about the baby, more than anything. But she drove to the hospital to check up on her—the wrong one, as it turned out. Of course she blamed Lexi for that. But at least she made an effort, for once. I have to give her some credit.

I wake the following morning to the sound of my phone ringing. Lexi's face flashes onto the screen. I sit up and hurriedly swipe my finger across it. "Honey! Are you okay?"

"Yeah. Just a bit shook up."

"I can catch a flight home this morning—"

"No! Don't! I'm fine. You're not going to come back for five little stitches. You're Tom's best man. He needs you there. I'll see you tomorrow as planned."

"Are you sure you'll be okay on your own until then?"

"Positive. I'm going to hunker down in the house today and take it easy. Maybe do some baby shopping on

Amazon." She hesitates, her face pinched. "I need to order some new maternity clothes anyway."

My stomach twists. "Did Price get back with you, yet?"

"He called me last night. The hospital filed a police report on the attack, so I told them to talk to Price in case it was connected to the other incidents. He said Wade and Helen were out of town for a couple of days visiting relatives, but he finally got a hold of Wade yesterday. He denied knowing anything about the vandalism, claimed he'd never been inside our house, which is true. We've only ever had Helen over a couple of times for coffee by herself."

"That doesn't mean he didn't trespass. Did Price check his record?"

"Yes. I have a copy of it right here: *shoplifting, assault and battery, theft by check, disorderly conduct, possession of a controlled substance, and driving while license suspended.*"

"All around loser. I figured as much. I wouldn't put anything past him. Did you get a look at the man who attacked you?"

"No, he was wearing a beanie and shades. He came at me from behind. It all happened so quickly. I was in shock, and he ran off right away."

"So it's possible it could have been Wade?"

There's a long pause before Lexi responds. "I suppose someone could have paid him to attack me."

9

CASH

The guys and I spend Saturday kart-racing and golfing, then head back to the hotel to shower up before dinner and a show. I check in with Lexi several times throughout the course of the day, heartened to hear she's having fun putting together an Amazon baby shower wish list, but nervous of the danger that could be lurking next door now that Wade is back. I'm tempted to take Jess up on her offer to check in on Lexi, but I know it wouldn't go over well—not when she's convinced it was Jess who sent me those messages and the suggestive T-shirt. Even if she's right, there's no way Jess would have hired Wade or anyone else to attack her. Jess doesn't have a cruel bone in her body.

When I wake the following morning, another slew of texts awaits me—this time from Lexi: *call me when you get this ... I'm so sorry!*

My chest tightens like it's in a vise and I'm half-afraid I'm going to have a heart attack as I jump out of bed and snatch up my phone. "Hey, what's going on? Are you okay?"

"Oh, Cash, I—" Lexi promptly bursts into tears, and I

clutch the phone tighter in my fist, a sinking feeling in my stomach. She sounds like she's hyperventilating. "Honey, calm down! Take a breath. Tell me what's wrong. Did someone try to break in?"

"I ... I ... I ... lost the baby last night," she blubbers.

I feel like I've just entered an eternal winter in Narnia. My lips freeze shut, my phone locked in a death grip in my icy fingers.

"Cash? Are you there?"

"I'm ... so sorry," I say, at last. "What happened?"

"I woke up at midnight with cramps." She chokes back another sob. "The doctor thinks it was probably the shock of the attack that triggered it."

I clench my fists, my thoughts racing around inside my pounding head. Anger wells up at the sheer injustice of it. Whoever attacked Lexi is responsible for killing our unborn child too. I won't stop until I find out who it was and give them what they have coming to them. I will be the husband Lexi deserves, even if it means severing all ties with Jess.

"Cash? Are you still there?" Lexi's voice is faint, wavering like a child unsure of herself.

"Yeah, I'm here."

"It was ... a little boy."

THE ATMOSPHERE among the guys on the flight home is subdued. Between the hangovers some of us are nursing, and the news about Lexi's attack and subsequent miscarriage, no one is in the mood to crack jokes. When we touch down in LAX, Tom squeezes my shoulder in parting. "So sorry, bro. Let me know if there's anything I can do."

"Appreciate it. I feel bad about putting a downer on your bachelor weekend."

"Naw, man. Not your fault. Go home and give Lexi a big hug from all of us."

THE MINUTE I walk through the door, Lexi collapses in my arms, her deep, guttural sobs rending my heart in two. I'm filled with a leaden mixture of sorrow, and guilt—sorrow that we lost a son, and guilt for ever wishing it had been Jess who was pregnant with my child to begin with. Maybe it's my fault this happened—a just punishment for my terrible thoughts. Could they be construed as betrayal, an emotional affair of sorts?

I kiss the top of Lexi's head and rock her in my arms on the couch until she stills. When she finally sits up and dries her eyes, I smooth her blonde hair gently back from her pale face. "I'll make us some tea," I say, getting to my feet. It always seems to soothe her.

As I'm filling the kettle, my phone beeps on the coffee table. Lexi picks it up and glances at the screen. "It's—" She breaks off and jerks her head toward me with a mixture of disbelief and horror on her face.

My stomach begins to churn. *Please don't let it be another message from an unknown number.*

"What's wrong? Who is it?" I ask, walking over to her.

Wordlessly, she hands me my phone. The look of disgust she gives me sends a shiver down my spine. *What now?*

I read the words on the screen twice, crinkling my brow in confusion: *It's a match!* Beneath the phrase, a stunning couple stares adoringly into each other's eyes, arms entwined.

"Platinum Pairs—really, Cash?" Lexi's tone has taken on a frosty edge and the hurt in her eyes has morphed into anger. "Do you want to tell me what you're doing on a dating app?"

I swipe frantically at the screen as it dawns on me what I'm looking at. "Wait a minute! I didn't sign up for this. This must be some kind of spam message." I toss my phone on the coffee table and curl my fingers into a fist in frustration. "Maybe Tom did this as some kind of groomsmen gag."

"It's not spam," Lexi counters. "They can't send you a match unless you have a profile with them."

"Well, I don't!"

Lexi reaches for her laptop on the couch next to her and flips it open. She taps steadily for a minute or two, then turns the screen around to face me. "Sure looks like a profile to me."

I stare disbelievingly at the photo that is undeniably me, dressed in a casual short-sleeved khaki shirt and shorts, grinning at the camera. An uneasy feeling goes through me. Jess took that photo of me on our first weekend away together in Charleston, South Carolina. "I didn't sign up for this site, Lexi. You have to believe me. I've never seen it before in my life. I'll email them right now and get this deleted."

She shakes her head slowly. "I don't know what to believe. Between this, and Jess showing up the other night like that—acting like you two had never been apart. Why didn't you tell me you were still in contact with her?"

I throw up my hands. "If that's what you call the odd text here and there. We were good friends once. That's all there is to it. She's pursuing her career, and I'm here with you."

Lexi chews on her lip for a moment. Her eyes glisten and I can tell she's fighting hard not to cry. "That's not what your mother told me the other night. She said you and Jess are still really close."

"Mom just likes to stir the pot, you know what she's like."

"Then you won't mind if I read your *odd message or two* to Jess, will you?"

Before I can stop her, Lexi swipes my phone from the coffee table and scrolls through it. Her expression darkens as she reads aloud, "*We need to talk. Meet me in 30 at our usual spot?*" She looks up sharply. "You're meeting her behind my back, too?"

"It's not like that. It was a one-off thing. I needed to confront her about those messages, that's all. I wanted to ask her directly. I figured I'd know if she was lying to my face."

Lexi's eyes fill with tears. "I guess I'm not that good. I can't tell when *you're* lying to my face."

I groan inwardly. I could kick myself for doing this to her right after she's lost the baby. She looks so sad, and I don't know how to comfort her. We're still getting to know one another with all our quirks, habits, and triggers, and I feel like I'm riding a bumper car when it comes to navigating Lexi's fragile emotions. It was different with Jess—refreshingly uncomplicated. We got one another. But Lexi's a riddle I don't know how to solve.

"Honey, please don't cry. There's nothing going on between me and Jess."

"Apparently, she doesn't think so. Why else would she have sent you that T-shirt? *Think of me when you wear this. Miss you babe!* She's sending a message loud and clear. She's never going away!"

I work my jaw side-to-side as an image of the expensive Montblanc pen stashed at the back of my desk drawer flashes to mind. That message was loud and clear too—*write me back into your future.* Is Jess having buyer's remorse after signing up for her PhD and sacrificing our relationship in the process? Maybe when she found out Lexi was pregnant, it changed her perspective on things. We were good together, and she knows it. I can't help thinking about what she said to me in the tavern that night: *It's not that I didn't want you.* Maybe, in a moment of irrational regret, jealousy got the better of her and she spray-painted that message on our wall and bleach-bombed Lexi's maternity clothes.

Am I crazy for thinking that? She seemed so concerned for Lexi when I told her how frightened she was—even offering to check up on her while I was in Vegas. What if I mistook morbid delight in Lexi's terror for sympathy? Lexi isn't as emotionally resilient as Jess. Maybe Jess sensed weakness and went in for the kill—even going so far as to hire someone to stab her in the park.

Kill. I shudder at the word—it's a sobering reminder that whoever is behind this killed my son. Lexi's words burn in my brain: *Someone could have paid Wade to attack me.*

I grimace as I take my weeping wife in my arms. I will make that someone pay for their crimes— even if it turns out to be Jess.

Cash has taken a couple of days off work to look after me as I recover, which is his way of trying to make up for lying to me about seeing Jess behind my back. I don't believe for a minute it was a one-off thing. Eleanor's no dummy—she sees how close they still are—she tried to warn me in her twisting-the-knife kind of way. Despite all Jess's denials, I'm convinced she would like nothing more than to get her claws back into my husband, and he's too weak to resist. Even the mention of her name lights a flame inside him he's powerless to extinguish.

"I made you breakfast," Cash says, breezing into the room holding a tray aloft. He feels awful about the fake profile on the dating site—which he adamantly denies signing up for—although, when I suggested Jess might have done it to antagonize me, he wasn't buying that either. Eleanor's not technologically savvy enough to set up a fake profile. I don't know who else he thinks would go to all that trouble to drive a wedge between us.

Despite all the tears and arguing, I can't help but reward him with a smile when I see all the effort he's gone to this morning. A tiny bud vase with a sprig from the garden garnishes the tray, alongside a China teacup and saucer, and a cinnamon scone from my favorite bakery. "The mail, m'lady," he announces with a flourish, tossing a handful of envelopes onto the bed next to me.

"You're going to make me lazy," I say with a chuckle, as he sets the tray on the bedside cabinet. "Or so your mother told me when she called to check up on me earlier. She was appalled to hear I was still in bed."

"You're not being lazy. You're healing," he says, kissing my fingers softly before clambering onto the bed and lying down next to me. He folds his arms behind his head and closes his eyes. "I could get used to a daytime nap myself."

I take a sip of tea and sigh with satisfaction. "Just how I like it, piping hot with a shot of honey."

"I aim for perfection," Cash mumbles sleepily.

I reach for the mail and sort through it. "Bill, bill, junk mail, bill." I hesitate when I come to a large, square envelope. We've received several condolence cards already—one from Tom, one from Chase's work colleagues, and one from Eleanor, in which she ignored me entirely: *So sorry for your loss, son.* Of course, I burst into tears the minute I read it. In an act of solidarity, Cash ripped it in two and tossed it in the trash. To his credit, he's made it clear to her that she's not to come over to our house anymore without an express invitation, so at least I won't have to deal with her face-to-face.

I open the envelope and slide the card out, studying the image of a cherub on the front. Beneath it, the message reads: *Too beautiful for earth.* "We have another condolence card," I say quietly.

"Who's it from?" Cash asks.

"The girls I work with. They all signed it. It says: *always remember I'm watching over you until we can be together again."* I pass the card to him. "That was sweet of them."

Cash studies it, a crestfallen look on his face. "Yeah, it was."

I reach for another envelope and hand it to him. "This one's addressed to you. Probably from your mother, just in case I didn't get the slight in the first one."

"Looks like you're spared the wrath of Eleanor this time. This isn't her handwriting," Cash says wryly, ripping open the envelope. He pulls out a card and I hear a sharp intake of breath.

"What is it?"

"Nothing," he says, sitting up abruptly.

"Who's it from?"

He makes a half-hearted attempt to stuff the card back in the envelope. "I don't know."

I narrow my eyes at him and hold out my hand, gesturing for the card. "Is it from Jess? Let me see!"

"Lexi, you don't want to do this," he says, in a pained tone.

"I'm sick and tired of you hiding things from me, Cash! Give it to me! Now!"

He huffs out a sigh before handing it over.

I frown at the word plastered across the front of the card beneath a large bottle of popped champagne: *Congratulations!* Flipping it open, I stare grimly at the handwritten message inside: *You dodged a bullet!*

"Why would someone send you a card congratulating you on dodging a bullet?" I turn to Cash, my bottom lip trembling. "You don't think ... they don't mean ... the baby, do they?"

Cash grabs the card from me and crumples it in his fist, evading eye contact. "Of course not. Tom probably sent it to all the guys to gig them after his bachelor weekend—you know how it is, to get the wives riled up."

"That's hardly appropriate—he knows we just lost our baby."

"Of course, he mailed it without thinking. Bet he's kicking himself now."

I pick at the stitching on the duvet. "Call him up and ask him if he sent it."

Cash lets out a nervous snort. "I'm not going to embarrass the poor guy even more."

"We need to know if it was him," I insist. "If it wasn't, we have to add this to the log we're keeping for Price."

Cash rubs a hand over his jaw, clearly torn between not wanting to upset me and not wanting to involve his best buddy in this burgeoning nightmare. He'd better make the right choice this time, because I'm growing tired of taking a back seat in his world.

"Fine," he says at length, pulling out his phone. "I'll ask him." He moves into the bathroom to make the call so I can only make out the odd muffled phrase every now and then. He reemerges a few minutes later, poker-faced. "It wasn't Tom, or any of the other guys."

"I didn't think so," I say, rubbing my temples. "It's more like the kind of sick thing your mother might do, but she's already sent us a spite-filled card, so we can rule her out."

"It wasn't spite-filled," Cash grumbles. "It was a sympathy card."

"Really? *So sorry for your loss, son.* I'm the one who miscarried," I say, jabbing a finger at my sternum, "and she didn't even mention me! That's passive-aggressive spite in all its inglorious colors!"

Cash sighs. "It was thoughtless, I'll give you that. But you have to understand she's always been overly protective of me. You know Dad left when I was six. It's been only the two of us all these years. She has no one else."

"And she never will so long as she treats your wife like the dirt beneath her shoes!" I yell. My shoulders shake as rage freefalls through me, and I bury my face in my hands in a bid to contain it.

Cash resumes his place next to me on the bed and pulls me into his arms. "Shhh, it's okay," he soothes.

"It's not okay! I hate that I keep crying over everything," I say between sobs.

"It's just the hormones," Cash says. "Anya went through the same thing when she was pregnant with Mila."

I bristle at the mention of Anya. Everything in our house is a daily reminder of my predecessor and her superior taste. "Cash, I don't think I'm up to having Mila here next week. It's too hard so soon after losing the baby."

He stops stroking my hair. "But I haven't seen her for a month-and-a-half. They just got back from Europe."

I dab at my eyes with a corner of the sheet. "I know. I'm trying, I really am, but I'm a hot mess right now. I don't want to scare Mila by bursting into tears at some cute little thing she comes out with—knowing we'll never get to hear our son say his first word. Can't we skip this week? You get her every other week."

A flicker of a frown crosses Cash's brow. "Okay, I'll talk to Mom about it. Maybe Mila can stay with her, and I can go over there to see her. We'll figure something out."

"Thanks," I say, sniffing as I wipe the tears from my cheeks. "I just need a few more days to sort myself out. I'm still trying to process everything." I trace my fingers lightly over the raised scar on my arm—an ugly reminder of the knife attack I endured.

The expression on Cash's face softens. He raises my arm to his lips and kisses my stitches. "You're safe now, Lexi. No one's going to hurt you again."

I give a dubious nod, knowing full well he can't give me that kind of guarantee—not when there's someone out there bent on getting what they want at any cost.

Jess won't win in the end. She may want what I have, but she's not getting my husband.

12

LEXI

True to his word, Cash makes arrangements for Mila to stay at Eleanor's house for the week. He goes over there every day after work, eats dinner with them, and spends a few hours playing with Mila, with my full backing. I would never try to come between him and his daughter. It's not Mila I'm afraid of losing my husband to. I tried again to convince Cash that the congratulations card must have come from Jess, but he refuses to entertain the idea. He doesn't want me sharing my suspicions with Price either. He says we should let the police do their job and not cast aspersions on anyone. It cuts to the core to know that, at all costs, he's trying to protect Jess like he's her knight in shining armor. It's me he should be worried about.

"How's Miss Mila doing today?" I ask brightly as he comes through the door late on Friday evening. The last thing I want to do is start the weekend out with an argument.

"Bursting with endless energy as usual. After forty rounds of *Go Fish*, I can't say the same for myself," he replies, flopping into an armchair.

"Will Anya pick her up from your mom's tomorrow?"

"I hope so."

"What's that supposed to mean?" I ask, picking up on a beat of hesitation in his tone.

He sighs. "I just hope she's not going to be difficult and change the schedule again at the last minute to spite me. She's still mad because I wouldn't keep Mila for the six weeks she and Anton were touring through Europe. From what Mila's told me, they spent a fair chunk of their time on the trip arguing. Reading between the lines, I think Anton was mad they had a six-year-old cramping their style the entire time."

I bite my bottom lip. "I'm sorry. You can blame me for that."

"Don't say that! It wasn't your fault. We were newly married. I wasn't going to put that on you. If they can afford to vacation abroad in five-star hotels for six weeks at a stretch, then it's up to them to figure out childcare."

"But you did tell them you would have Mila when they booked the trip originally. I can understand why they didn't take it too well when you announced you were getting married and reneged on the deal."

Cash gives an irritated shrug. "We all have to adapt. I had to when Anya ran off with Anton. If he's not interested in having a daughter, he shouldn't have married Anya. Everyone knows a single mother's a package deal." He drums his fingers on the arm of his chair. "I just hope their marriage isn't in trouble. Some of the things Mila's been saying since she got back concern me. I don't want to see her bouncing from one broken home to the next."

I walk around to the back of the armchair and begin massaging his neck. "You're a good dad, you know that?

Don't worry about Anya—she's a big girl, she can look after herself. How about a glass of wine to relax before dinner?"

Cash smiles gratefully up at me. "I'd love one. How are you doing?"

"Better. I cleaned the bathrooms today, did some laundry, and I haven't cried in the past sixty minutes, so that's a record."

Cash squeezes my hand. "How about we curl up on the couch together and watch a movie later—does a comedy sound good?"

WE'RE both laughing uncontrollably at Steve Martin's facial expressions later that evening, when our phones start pinging in unison on the counter where we left them to charge.

"I'd better check and make sure that's not Mom calling about Mila," Cash says, getting to his feet. When he picks up his phone, his face pales.

"Is everything all right?" I call over to him.

Instead of responding, he picks up my phone and holds both screens side-by-side. "Someone texted us both the same message."

I get to my feet and walk over to where he's standing. Frowning, I peer down at the phones in his hand and read the duplicate text on the screens: *Ignoring me makes me angrier.*

I gasp, my fingers digging into Cash's arm. "Should we text them back?"

He twists his lips. "No. Ignoring them is exactly what we need to do. I'm going to turn off my phone, and you should too."

. . .

It's after midnight by the time we tumble into bed after downing a bottle of wine between us—most of which Cash consumed. Predictably, he falls asleep right away, his rhythmic breathing ebbing and flowing like clockwork. Sleep has never come quite as easily for me, but at some point, I doze off.

A loud banging on the door awakens me in the early hours. I sit bolt upright in bed, blinking myself awake. Cash throws aside the duvet and climbs out of bed. "I'll get it. Stay here!"

"Please be careful!" I say, drawing my knees up to my chin as he jogs down the stairs.

I hear the sound of voices conversing in urgent tones at the front door. Moments later, Cash pounds his way back up to the bedroom. He goes straight to the dresser and starts pulling out clothes in a frenzy. "That was the police."

I throw back the covers on the bed and jump to my feet. "The *police*? What's going on?"

"There was a fire at Mom's," he says, pulling a long-sleeved shirt over his head.

I suck in a hard breath. "Are they ... are your mom and Mila okay?"

"No one was hurt, but Mom's in shock. I need to get over there right away. She's not making much sense. She says Mila's not with her."

13

CASH

Undulating waves of panic knead my chest as I drive. I alternate between berating myself and reassuring myself that Mila is safe. I shouldn't have turned off my phone last night. It was irresponsible of me, knowing Mila was alone with my mom. I just wanted to have one evening when I didn't have to worry about another random message upsetting Lexi. The truth is, I've been getting an increasing number of texts from various unknown numbers. I haven't responded to any of them, but they're becoming creepier and more unhinged with every iteration: *I will destroy your life, you look good in that blue shirt, I can take care of her, she belongs in a cage, I watch you when you sleep, you need me, she's planning to poison you, you're dead to me.*

Whoever is behind the messages is seriously deranged, shifting between loving me and hating me, wanting to kill me one minute, and my wife the next. At this point, I'm not sure which of us is in more danger. Maybe I should pass my suspicions about Jess on to Officer Price. Could she have a bone to pick with me about how quickly I moved on? If she has become unhinged, my life and Lexi's could be at stake. Lexi doesn't know that I met up with Jess briefly after visiting Mila at Mom's last night. I wanted to confront her again about the plethora of vile text messages. She was adamant it wasn't her, hurt and angry that I could even suspect her after our previous conversation, and we parted on a discordant note, her face a mask of indignation. I've never seen that side of her before. Could repressed jealousy and anger have combusted into a campaign of revenge and retribution? I've never known Jess to have a violent streak, but I suppose it's possible she could have paid someone to stab Lexi. Maybe the intention was to kill her, but it didn't pan out. If that's the case, she might make another attempt. The thought sends an arctic chill through my veins. I grip the steering wheel tighter and accelerate.

For now, I need to stay focused on locating Mila. I've tried calling Anya but she's not picking up. Maybe it's just as well. There's no sense in alarming her before I know for sure what the situation is. I got conflicting accounts from the police officer I spoke to a few minutes ago. The paramedics gave Mom a sedative, which might explain her confusion. Hopefully, she'll be more coherent by the time I get there. She told the police she thinks Mila is with one of the neighbors, but she can't remember which one, or if they picked Mila up, or if she took her over there. The uncertainty terrifies me. The police are going door-to-door looking for my daughter right now. The firefighters have confirmed she's not anywhere in the house passed out from smoke inhalation, but that doesn't make me feel any better. What if she's not with a neighbor? What if she's been abducted? I growl in frustration, revving the engine impatiently as I wait for the traffic light in front of me to turn green.

I can't shake the hideous thought that the fire might

have something to do with everything else that's been happening. I don't want to believe that someone tried to murder my family, but what else am I supposed to think? I'm a numbers guy by trade, and the odds are not in favor of the fire being a coincidence. Whoever's behind this is growing increasingly desperate for attention. I've been doing my best to ignore them, hoping they would tire of harassing us, but they warned us it would only make them angrier. They've got my attention now. A cold sweat trickles down the back of my neck. It's clear they'll stop at nothing. They attacked my wife, murdered my son, and tried to kill my mother and daughter—they might even have abducted Mila for all I know.

When I finally screech to a halt outside my mother's house after what seems like an unending drive, the fire has already been put out. Several firefighters are still milling around packing up equipment. I jump out and jog across the lawn to them. "Hey! I'm Cash Reisinger, the homeowner's son. Where is she—where's Eleanor?"

"We took her next-door to her neighbor's house," one of the men responds. "She was pretty shook up."

"And her granddaughter?"

The firefighter throws me a puzzled look. "Sir, there was only one occupant in the house. You might want to talk to the police if you have any questions."

My heart seizes in my chest. This isn't making any sense. Where's Mila? Was the fire merely a diversion so someone could sweep in and take her? Panic sears a path through my gut. If this is Jess's doing, I'll tear her limb from limb if she harms my daughter. I turn on my heel and dash to the nearest neighbor's house. I have to get to the bottom of this before it's too late. There's a light on, so I don't hesitate to ring the doorbell repeatedly. At last, my mother's elderly neighbor, Dirk, opens his front door, blinking fearfully into the darkness.

"It's me, Cash," I blurt out.

"Ah, Cash! Come on in. Eleanor's having a lie down on the couch right now."

I follow Dirk as he ushers me at an agonizingly ponderous pace into the family room where my mother is stretched out on a faded, chintz couch, looking strangely vulnerable for once.

"Mom! Where's Mila?"

She sits up slowly, blinking at me with a dazed expression. "Mila? Didn't anyone tell you?"

My stomach churns another full circle. "Tell me what?"

She traces a hand across her brow. "In all the chaos, I'd forgotten that Anya came by yesterday at bedtime and picked her up. She said she had to work today and needed to drop her off early at a friend's house." She presses her lips together. "I hope I didn't scare you. I can't remember what I told the firefighters. I couldn't think straight earlier—being woken out of my sleep like that by the fire alarm, and then the house was full of smoke. It was terrible. I don't know what happened. I'm always so diligent about blowing out my candles before I go to bed."

The leaden weight of fear I've been carrying falls from my shoulders. I was worried Mila might have been abducted by the lunatic who's been wreaking havoc on my life, but it turns out there was a simple explanation all along. She's with her mother—perfectly safe. I scrub my hands over my face, unable to keep a smile from breaking out. It's hard not to become paranoid under the circumstances—interpreting everything that happens as part of an evil plot some nutcase is weaving into our lives. I should be irritated that Anya has, yet again, brazenly ignored our custody agreement to suit her schedule. But, for once, I'm grateful she picked Mila up early. I can't bear to picture my daughter waking up in her grandmother's house to the terrifying sound of crackling flames and the noxious smell of smoke.

"Would you like a coffee, Cash?" Dirk asks. "Or a finger of whisky, perhaps?"

"No thanks. I'm fine," I reply, sinking down on the couch next to my mother. I give her a remonstrative grin. "Maybe now you'll start using those flameless candles I gave you last Christmas. They don't have a scent, but they look like the real thing."

My mother presses a veined hand to her cheek. "That's the strange part about it. It turns out it wasn't my candles that started the fire. They're telling me it was arson." She blinks at me in a discomposed manner. "Who would do such a thing, darling?"

14

CASH

Our initial harassment report has been elevated from non-threatening to critical status. The deliberate torching of my mother's house, along with the steady stream of increasingly disturbing messages, the knife attack on Lexi, and the various random acts of trespassing and vandalism have finally forced the police to take the situation seriously.

I squeeze Lexi's hand as we take a seat opposite Price in his stuffy office at the station. She's been a rock over the past few hours, even agreeing, albeit reluctantly, to let Mom—who's clearly shell-shocked—stay with us for a few days until the arson investigator has finished up at her house.

Price clears his throat. "Let's go over this one more time. Can you think of anyone you might have fallen out with, or who might have threatened you in the past—even indirectly—neighbors, work colleagues, tradespeople who've done work at your house?"

"No. I can't think of anyone," I say, glancing across at Lexi for confirmation.

She shakes her head. "I can't think of anyone either.

Most of the messages are directed at Cash. I don't have any enemies."

"You do now," I say grimly.

"Any idea what they want?" Price asks, fingering the folds on his double chin.

"They want my husband," Lexi blurts out. "And they want me out of the way. That's obvious. It's the recurring theme in all the messages."

I swallow, before nodding in agreement. It's terrifying to admit that someone is trying to kill my wife. It's even more terrifying to think I might know who that person is.

Price audits me with a keen gaze. "So why would this person set fire to your mother's house?"

I shrug. "Beats me. To punish me, perhaps? Whoever it is, they're willing to hurt anyone close to me to let me know they're not messing around. Maybe the fire was just for attention. They don't like being ignored, and I'm not giving them the attention they want. They've bombarded my phone with all sorts of other vile messages, but I haven't responded to any of them."

Price thumbs through the notebook on the desk in front of him. "I have a record of everything you've sent me. I'll review it and see if anything sticks out. Going back to the initial list of suspects, I want to revisit some of these names you gave me." He interlinks his fingers in front of him and rests them on his considerable belly. "Let's assume for a minute, as the messages seem to indicate, this is someone you had some kind of relationship with, Cash. I think we can rule out your next-door-neighbor, Wade Banks—unless ... there's something I'm missing?" He peers at me quizzically.

My cheeks heat up and I give a vehement shake of my

head. "I've barely spoken more than a few sentences to the man in all the time I've lived there."

Price taps a beefy finger on his desk. "So that leaves your ex-girlfriend and your ex-wife. Unless there's anyone else who might have a bone to pick with either of you?"

"His mother hates me," Lexi pipes up. "She's made it abundantly clear she wishes I wasn't in his life. She doesn't think I'm good enough for him."

I throw Lexi an irritated look. "I hardly think she would have set fire to her own house."

"I didn't say she did," Lexi replies, folding her arms in front of her. "I'm just alluding to the fact that she doesn't like me—she tries to undermine me every chance she gets."

Price makes a point of coughing into his fist. "She seems to be of the opinion it's you who dislikes her. When I spoke to her earlier, she insinuated you might have been behind the fire."

"That's ridiculous!" I interrupt. "Lexi and I were asleep in bed last night until the police knocked on our door."

Lexi lets out a dejected sigh. "I've done everything I can to make the relationship with Cash's mother work, but she's bent on destroying it. It wouldn't surprise me if she set fire to her own house just so she could blame it on me."

Price purses his lips. "Family wrangling aside, it's unlikely she's the arsonist. Are there any other people you can think of who might have it in for you?"

"What about someone from your past?" I ask Lexi, Jess's suggestion coming back to mind.

She frowns. "Why would someone from my past pretend to be an ex who wants you back?"

I shrug. "I don't know—to get back at you for something. To make you jealous."

"I have to agree the theory doesn't hold much merit."

Price taps his fingers on the notebook in front of him. "I think we need to zero in on the more obvious pool of candidates. Judging from the messages, it's most likely a woman from Cash's past. We'll start there. We can widen the search once we eliminate anyone with an alibi." He clears his throat again before adding, "I'll need the contact information for your exes."

A jolt of trepidation goes through me as I write it down on the pad of paper he pushes across the table to me. "My ex-wife's at work so she may not answer," I tell him.

"It's not his ex-wife who's been inserting herself into our lives anyway," Lexi says, throwing me an annoyed look. "It's his ex-girlfriend you should be focusing on."

"I wouldn't go that far," I say, shifting uncomfortably in my seat.

"Really?" Lexi raises her brows. "Showing up at our house uninvited, meeting you behind my back, sending you gifts, telling you how much she wants you back, threatening me, leaving deranged messages, not to mention vandalizing our house. Everything points to Jess. You're in denial about her. Don't you care that she might have tried to kill your own mother and child?"

"I admit it doesn't look good," Cash acknowledges, "but I'm having a hard time wrapping my head around the idea that Jess could be that vindictive."

"I've seen it all. You'd be shocked how low people can go when they lead with emotion," Price says, getting to his feet. "I'll pay your exes a visit and see what they have to say for themselves. That's all I need from you, for now. If you think of anyone else I should speak with, let me know."

Lexi and I walk back out to the car in silence. I'm not sure how I feel about her so forcefully airing her suspicions about Jess, but I can hardly fault her. I slide into the driver's seat, and slam the car door shut, determined not to let it come between us. We need to keep a united front. "Are you still up for Mom coming to stay with us for a few days? Dirk said she could stay at his place if she wants, but she's not comfortable with that idea."

"Yes, of course." Lexi replies, laying a placating hand on my arm. "I wasn't trying to imply that your mother burned down her own house. That would be ridiculous. I was only trying to answer Price's question honestly. She has a caustic tongue when it comes to me. It's hard to believe anything other than that she despises me."

I grimace as I turn on the ignition. "Can't argue with that. It sounds as if she's been badmouthing you to Price, as well. Hopefully, she can be civil for a few days until she goes back to her own house."

Lexi sighs as she clicks her seatbelt into place. "I'm more concerned about what Jess is going to do next. I know you don't want to believe she's behind any of this, but, more and more, I'm convinced it's her. She could have hired someone to do her dirty work for her—Wade, who knows? Maybe she told him to make your life miserable and he went further than she intended. Or maybe Price is right, and her emotions got the better of her and, in a moment of blind rage, she decided she wanted us all dead—even your daughter. You never really know what someone's capable of until they're pushed to their limits."

I swerve out of the parking lot too quickly, disturbed by the thought that Mila could easily have been there when the fire was started—maybe that was the intention. "You're right. I need to take my blinders off when it comes to Jess. I'm sorry if I created a jealous monster by staying in touch with her," I say, in the hopes of shutting down the conversation. My head's spinning and I don't want to argue with Lexi, but

I'm still having a hard time believing Jess has gone off the rails entirely. She's always been levelheaded. Unless there's something I've been missing all along.

MY MOTHER OPENS the door to us with a full face of makeup and a disapproving frown. "You're late," she says, running her hooded eyes over Lexi as if to pinpoint the source of our tardiness. "My bags are right here. Everything smells of smoke, so I'll need to do laundry as soon as I get to your place."

Evidently, she's made a rapid recovery from her state of catatonic shock. I roll my eyes when I see how much stuff she's planning on bringing with her, but I know better than to comment on it. It won't change a thing, even if I spend the next fifteen minutes trying to reason with her.

"Not a problem, Eleanor. Everything in our house is at your disposal," Lexi says, helping her to the car. "We want you to make yourself at home while you're with us."

Mom sniffs as she reaches for her seatbelt. "I suppose you're still lounging around the house feeling sorry for yourself."

"Actually, I go back to work on Monday," Lexi answers with a tight smile. "You'll have the place to yourself during the day."

I grit my teeth as I pull away from the curb. This is starting out about as well as I predicted.

Mom lets out a humph. "I hope you're not expecting me to clean up after you."

I shoot her a warning look in the rearview mirror. She turns away and stares out the window for the remainder of the ride home.

After I've lugged her bags up to the guest room, I head

back downstairs to join her and Lexi in the kitchen. I pause on the bottom step when I hear raised voices.

"Don't think I don't know what you're up to—trying to cut me out of my son's life. I wouldn't put it past you to be the arsonist!" my mother hisses.

"And I wouldn't put it past you to set fire to your own house—anything to get Cash's attention," Lexi volleys back. "You've always resented me taking him away from you!"

"You're putting his life in danger. You're the reason he's getting those threatening messages. I know all about them. I found them on his phone."

"*I'm* putting his life in danger? It's Jess you should be talking to! She's the crazy one!"

My mother's voice rises a notch. "You brought this on him—flaunting yourself and your pregnancy all over Facebook, trying to get a rise out of her."

"It's hardly my fault his demented ex is threatening him!" Lexi replies.

"At least she was worth his time. You've given him nothing, not even a child!" my mother retorts. "And, believe me, that's the *only* reason he married you!"

15

LEXI

"She can't stay here!" I yell at Cash. "Either she goes, or I go. I'm sorry, I really am. I was willing to try, but she's not even making an effort. She's accusing me of stirring all this up just by existing! And she acts like it's my fault we lost the baby! How do you think that makes me feel?"

Cash rubs a hand over his creased brow. "I know. I'm sorry, honey. Can you please give her one more chance? She realizes she was out of line. She says she was stressed out about the fire. She's agreed to apologize."

"Apologize? How can you come back from something like that?" I fold my arms in front of me and glare at him. "I love you, Cash, but you expect the impossible of me. Your family dynamic with your mother is toxic. All your past relationships are hanging over us like a dark cloud. How can we have a future together when someone—maybe, all of them—are trying to destroy our marriage?" I bite back a sob. "We need to get away from here. I want us to start over someplace new."

Cash smooths his hands over his hair, closing his eyes

briefly. "I get it, I do. We can talk about it later. But first, I need to address the immediate problem of where Mom's going to sleep tonight. She can't stay in her own house. Thankfully, the damage is confined to the sunroom so she can move back in as soon as she gets the green light from the fire department. Can't we at least offer her a roof over her head for a few nights? You don't have to speak to her if you don't want to."

"I'm not asking you to put her out on the street," I reply. "Get her a hotel room."

Cash flinches. "That seems a bit heartless, considering what she's been through. She's traumatized."

I fling my arms wide in frustration. "I'm traumatized too! I was attacked and lost our baby, in case you've forgotten. She doesn't care about that though. It's all about egocentric Eleanor."

"All right," Cash says, in a resigned tone. "How about we let her stay here tonight and I'll figure out something else after that?"

I shrug. "Fine. Just don't expect me to be at her beck and call. I've had my fill of her abuse."

"You won't have to lift a finger. I'll take care of her," Cash promises.

TRUE TO HIS WORD, he keeps Eleanor out of my way for the rest of the day. I leave them to fix their own lunch while I make a much-needed grocery run. When I arrive home, I pick up the mail that's been lying untouched in our mailbox for several days and bring it into the house. "I could use some help unloading the car," I say to Cash, who's hunched over his laptop at the kitchen island.

"Sure," he replies, slamming the lid shut and jumping to

his feet. The speed at which he closed it puts me on high alert. Was he looking at something he didn't want me to see? "Where's your mom?" I ask, trying not to sound as prickly as I feel inside.

"Taking a nap in her room."

"What were you working on?" I venture, unable to curb my curiosity.

"Just taking care of a few emails," he replies, not meeting my gaze.

I know immediately he's hiding something. I'm unsure whether to press it any further or leave it for now. Despite everything that's gone down, I'm not naive enough to believe that he's cut off all communication with Jess, as he promised. He's like an addict when it comes to her—craving what he can't have, compelled to seek it out, regardless.

I taste acid in the back of my throat as I fight a losing battle to swallow my next question back down. "Were the emails from Jess?"

His face clouds over. "Leave it alone, Lexi. I'm going to grab the groceries out of the car."

"It's never going to end, is it?" I cry, riding the tide of emotion inside. "Do you like the idea that she wants you back, that we're both available to you? Does it give you some kind of macho ego boost?"

"Lexi, don't—"

"What on earth are you two arguing about now?" Eleanor interrupts, shuffling into the room in her pink, quilted slippers. "I don't know how you expect me to sleep when you insist on airing your dirty laundry twenty-four seven." She purses her lips. "Did I hear Jess's name mentioned?"

"Mom, please! This has nothing to do with you," Cash admonishes her.

I turn my back on her and reach for the mail I tossed on the counter. She makes no bones about ignoring me whenever she feels like it—maybe I should try doing the same. I rip open a small, lilac envelope and pull out a notecard.

"Who's that from?" Cash asks.

I study the big, yellow, smiley-face emoji on the front. It doesn't look like a run-of-the-mill condolence card. I flip it open and read the message: *I'm watching you!* I suck in a sharp breath, dropping it like it's contaminated.

Cash snatches the card up from the floor and stares at it, his expression hardening.

Eleanor blinks at him, eyebrows arched in expectation. "What is it, dear?"

"Nothing. Just another condolence card. They always upset Lexi."

He crams it into his back pocket and slides an arm around me. I keep shaking, but Cash's warm presence is reassuring.

"Really Lexi, there's no need to be so dramatic," Eleanor says, her voice dripping with censure. "I may as well go back to bed if you two can promise to keep your voices down."

The minute she disappears from view, I turn to Cash. "I've seen that card before."

He nods distractedly. "I'm sure they sell them all over."

I lower my voice to an urgent whisper. "I don't mean in a store. I saw a box of them at your mom's house."

16

CASH

Lexi is insisting we drive to my mother's house to look for a stupid box of cards. It's a fool's errand I've been trying to talk her out of for the past half hour, but she's convinced she saw them there the night we went over for dinner—although she can't remember exactly where. I know she's really shaken up, but she's mistaken about the cards. My mother would rather walk on hot coals than deign to buy anything with a yellow smiley face on it.

Understandably, Lexi's a basket case of emotions after everything she's gone through, which only makes her more paranoid. She's also deeply hurt by what my mother said about me marrying her because of the baby. She wants to believe what her mind's telling her—that my mother is behind the latest message meant to frighten her. I need to proceed with caution.

"Honey, Mom didn't send that card, if that's what you're thinking."

"How do you know?" Lexi fires back, pacing across the kitchen floor. "She hates my guts! She enjoys making me squirm."

I throw up my hands. "*I'm watching you.* Please! She's not that subtle. Mom says and does whatever she wants, whenever she wants—unfiltered. You know that as well as anyone. She'd rather insult you to your face and wallow in your reaction."

"You're too easily taken in by her. She'd do anything to scare me out of this marriage—including hiring someone to stab me!" Lexi rasps, jabbing a finger in my chest for emphasis.

I twist my lips in frustration. "First you tell me I'm underestimating Jess's jealousy, now I'm underestimating my mother's hatred. Which is it?"

Lexi breathes heavily through her nostrils for a moment or two, before responding. "What if they're in this together? I've had some time to think about it and it makes sense. What if they joined forces and hired Wade to stab me?"

I can't help but let out a derisive snort, even though I know better than to antagonize Lexi to the point of tears. "I'm not sure our pothead neighbor could pull himself up from the couch long enough to even walk to the park. This is beginning to sound more and more like a conspiracy theory."

"Don't you see what they're doing to us?" Lexi pleads. "This is exactly what they want—to make you think I'm crazy so they can destroy our relationship. And you're playing right into their hands by taking their side."

I raise my hands in defeat. "Fine. Get in the car. We'll drive to my mom's right now and look for those stupid cards. If that's what it's going to take to satisfy you that she hasn't hatched some evil plan with Wade and Jess to get rid of you, then that's what we'll do."

I make a quick call to Price to get permission to enter my mom's house, then leave a note on the kitchen table telling her we're running errands and will return shortly. With a bit of luck, we'll be back before she wakes up and realizes we've left her to fend for herself. I throw a sidelong glance at Lexi as I slide behind the wheel of my Audi and back down the driveway. Her ashen face is etched with worry. I'm not doing a good job of being an understanding spouse. I'm tired and frustrated myself—I can only imagine how she feels, right on the tail of suffering a miscarriage. I need to make a bigger effort to reassure her that we're a team.

"Look, I'm sorry for getting riled up back there," I say, as I pull onto the street. "I know it's tense with my mother in the house. I texted Tom earlier to ask if she could stay in his guest apartment for a couple of nights. He's offered to help in whatever way he can. He said he'll keep an eye on her for me."

"I hope you didn't tell him it was because I was being unreasonable," Lexi says, in a testy tone.

"Of course not," I say, keeping my eyes fixed on the road ahead. The truth is, I may not have been that diplomatic. I didn't tell Tom the full extent of it, but I hinted that he'd be sparing me a catfight.

My phone rings, preventing me from digging myself into an even bigger hole. "It's Price," I say, as I hit the speaker. "I wasn't expecting to hear back from him so soon."

"I'm afraid I don't have much to report," he begins. "Unfortunately, I haven't been able to meet with either your ex-wife or your ex-girlfriend, yet."

"I'm not surprised," I say. "They both work long hours."

"Apparently, your ex-wife was fired from her job a couple of days ago."

The traffic light up ahead turns red and I slow to a stop. My brain scrambles to catch up with the conversation.

"Fired? Are you sure? This is the first I'm hearing about it. What for?"

"The company wasn't able to divulge that information over the phone," Price replies. "I went by the address you gave me but there was no one home. I've tried calling her cell but she's not picking up."

The niggling feeling of disquiet in my stomach intensifies. Anya has been acting strangely. I'm afraid her relationship with Anton might be on the rocks, which will leave her in a bind thanks to the prenup she signed. And now she's gone and lost her job which means she'll be hitting me up for money. I frown as another thought occurs to me. If she lost her job a couple of days ago, why did she lie about needing to pick Mila up early from my mother's? Is it possible she knew there would be a fire there that night? Is my ex-wife involved? I blow out a heavy breath. I can't go there. I'm becoming as bad as Lexi with my conspiracy theories.

"I'll try reaching Anya once we hang up," I tell Price, as I accelerate through the intersection. "What about Jess? You said you couldn't reach her either."

He takes his sweet time before answering. "Her sister, Naomi, reported her missing last night. She says you were the last person to see her."

17

CASH

For a split second I lose focus, almost veering into the path of oncoming traffic.

"Look out!" Lexi yells, bringing me back to my senses in time to narrowly miss causing a collision with a delivery truck. A cacophony of beeps confirms the gravity of my lapse in concentration.

Sweat prickles across my hairline. I grip the steering wheel so tightly it feels like it might snap in two in my hands. Price must have misunderstood what Naomi said.

"That can't be right. She ... I mean—" I kill the thought before I can voice it. I know Jess isn't missing—she can't be. She texted me this morning. But I don't want Lexi to know about that. I need to think this through before I say anything—or possibly nothing. Either way I'll incriminate myself. The question is whether lying to Lexi, or to Price, is the lesser of two evils in this moment. The last thing I want is for my wife to find out I've been venting about her to Jess. Our relationship is under enough strain as it is. Last night, I sent Jess a long text apologizing for accusing her of harassing my wife. I even admitted I feel trapped at times and wonder if I made a mistake marrying Lexi so quickly. I ended up begging Jess to meet me at our special spot at the park. It was a lapse in judgement—another infamous spur-of-the-moment move on my end—but some part of me was hoping Jess would admit to regretting her decision to let me go. Not because I'm craving the ego boost of two women wanting me, like Lexi accused me of, but because I've never stopped loving Jess.

When she finally texted me back this morning, her message terrified me: *I wish she would disappear off the face of the earth.* I realized immediately I'd made a terrible mistake and deleted the entire thread. A cold shiver goes down my back. Somehow, I need to convince Price that Jess isn't missing, without incriminating myself in a sordid scheme to get rid of my wife. It's not Jess disappearing I'm afraid of—it's my wife I'm scared for. The threats are becoming all too real. If Lexi were ever to turn up missing, or dead, my dalliance with Jess is going to make me look like the guilty party. It's time I put an end to our warped relationship—not that there's anything to it other than an emotional cord I haven't cut, yet. At least, that's what I've been telling myself. The truth is, I'm beginning to question if it's really going to be that easy. What if I've created a monster—a Jess-yll and Hyde ex-girlfriend who'll stop at nothing to get me back?

"Cash, did you hear what Officer Price said?" Lexi's tense tone finally snaps me out of my cascading vortex of fear.

"Sorry. Traffic. I zoned out there for a minute."

Price coughs to reclaim my attention. "Naomi said Jess didn't come home after heading out to meet up with you last night. She hasn't responded to any of her texts either. Naomi also sent a group text out to Jess's friends. No one knows where she is."

I frown, trying to wrap my head around it. Jess and her

younger sister, Naomi—a student nurse—rent an apartment near the university where Jess is doing her PhD. It's out of character for Jess not to check in with Naomi. I quickly quash a flicker of jealousy at the thought that she might have been with another guy. That would explain why she didn't message me back until this morning. As soon as I get a moment to myself, I'll text her and ask her what she's playing at. I'm telling myself it's out of concern for Naomi, but I'm suddenly consumed with the need to know if Jess has met someone else—someone more important than the PhD she chose over me.

"I didn't meet her last night. I was home with Lexi all evening. Maybe she didn't want her sister knowing she was spending the night with some guy," I say, trying to sound unconcerned.

"Is that typical behavior for her?" Price asks. "To bunk at a stranger's house?"

I squirm under the intense scrutiny of Lexi's stare. "Well, not really, but it's possible."

After a stony silence, Price continues, "I'll need to take your statement down at the station."

"Uh, sure."

"The sooner, the better," he adds.

I hang up after agreeing to swing by on our way back from my mom's house. My heart races in my chest as I consider the implications. There's no way out of this quandary other than to come clean and show Price the text I got from Jess this morning. I can still pull it up in my deleted messages. Anything else I say is going to make it seem like I'm trying to hide something.

"Are you okay to drive? You look shook up," Lexi says, giving me an appraising once-over.

"Just frustrated," I reply, trying to shrug it off.

"Why would Naomi say you were the last one to see Jess?" Lexi persists.

I steel my features to neutral. I should have known Jess would tell Naomi about my text. Still, there's no need for Lexi to find out about it. I'll explain the situation to Price, show him Jess's response this morning, and clear everything up. Maybe she'll have resurfaced by then and this will be a moot issue anyway.

"No idea," I say. "She probably gave Price some names of people to talk to, that's all."

I pull into my mother's driveway and switch off the engine. "I guarantee you there are no smiley face cards lurking here. Let's get this over with and head to the station as quickly as we can."

From the front view of the house, the fire damage isn't visible, but the lingering smell of smoke in the air itches my nostrils the minute I exit the car. I unlock the front door and hold the caution tape aside so Lexi can step into the hallway.

She wrinkles her nose. "It stinks in here."

"I have a contractor lined up to start on the repairs next week," I tell her. "Once the burned materials are removed, we'll give the place a good airing out."

Lexi shoots me an alarmed look. "Does Tom know your mother is going to be staying with him that long?"

"She'll be out of his way in the guest apartment. He doesn't mind," I say dismissively. "Where do you think you saw those cards?"

Lexi frowns. "I'm not sure. Why don't you check the office and I'll look in your mom's bedroom?"

I grimace. "Please don't disturb anything. She'll freak out if she thinks we were going through her stuff."

"We can blame it on the arson investigator," Lexi replies, already heading down the hallway.

I push open the door to my mother's office and step inside, my mind racing ahead to my meeting with Officer Price. I wonder if he thinks I'm having an affair with Jess. What if he suspects me of helping her wage a campaign of terror against my wife? Things might not go as smoothly as I'm hoping. I need to think carefully about what to tell him.

I suck in an uneasy breath as I glance distractedly around the space. Mom's office is prim and orderly, as always. A floral pen in a gilt stand sits to one side of a scalloped writing pad. I half-heartedly scan the contents of the shelves, mainly so I can assure Lexi I did a thorough job: books, an assortment of knick-knacks, an antique glass vase, a small clock making an annoying ticking sound. No evidence that my mother is harassing my wife.

Not until I open the desk drawer and find myself staring back at a yellow smiley face.

"Find anything?" Lexi asks, sticking her head inside the office a few minutes later.

I make a show of rooting around in the cubbyholes above my mom's desk. "Nothing. How about you?"

"Not yet. But I know I saw those cards here somewhere," Lexi answers. "Maybe your mom moved them. Keep looking. I'll check the family room."

I draw my brows together in disapproval. "We don't have time to search the whole house. Price is expecting me to show up at the station any minute now to give a statement. And if we don't get back to the house soon, Mom will throw a fit."

Lexi puts a hand on her hip and scratches her forehead distractedly. "Okay, okay. Let me think for a minute. The cards were definitely in the house somewhere. I know for sure I saw them the night we came over for dinner." She lets out a gasp and swings around to face me. "I remember now! It was when I left the sonogram picture on your mom's desk. They were in here."

Before I can stop her, she yanks open the top desk

drawer. Her eyes widen and she lets out a vindicated squeal as she reaches inside for the box of smiley face cards. "Told you!" she says, shaking the box in my face. "I knew this was exactly the kind of sick stunt your mother would pull!"

I take it from her, willing it to magically disappear as I examine it. "Are you sure these are the same cards?"

Lexi snatches the box back from me and slips it into her jacket pocket. "We'll soon find out, won't we?" she says, marching out of the room.

I don't say much on the drive to the police station, choosing instead to gaze morosely through the windscreen as I reflect on what this means. It's not Mom's typical tactic —she specializes in tongue-lashings and verbal dressing-downs—but I can't deny anymore what she's done, with the evidence staring me in the face. She's stooped to a new low, and what if it's even worse? What if she's working with Jess in a bid to get rid of Lexi?

"You have to confront her now that we've caught her red-handed," Lexi says. "At a minimum, she's involved in what's been happening, and I wouldn't put it past her to have orchestrated the whole thing."

"You're jumping to conclusions," I say, scowling. "If she sent you the card, it was a petty thing to do, admittedly. But that might be the height of it."

It's a weak argument, I know, but I'm clinging to the hope that my mother simply saw an opportunity to add a little fuel to the fire, knowing we were being harassed by Jess. The idea that she could have coordinated an elaborate criminal campaign involving vandalism, arson, threats, and attempted murder is beyond comprehension.

"Besides, it's not her modus operandi," I add. "Like we talked about already, she thrives on in-your-face confronta-tion where she gets instant satisfaction."

"Maybe she wasn't getting the reaction she wanted and decided to up the ante," Lexi snaps.

I pull into the police station parking lot and rub my hand wearily over my face. "Do you want to wait here? This shouldn't take long."

"No. Are you crazy? I'm not staying in the car by myself —not even in a police parking lot," she answers tersely, as she unbuckles her seatbelt.

Inside the reception area, she plonks down unhappily on a plastic chair while a desk sergeant escorts me to an interview room.

"Thanks for getting here promptly," Price says, when he enters the room a moment later. "Time is always of the essence in these circumstances."

By *circumstances*, he means missing persons' cases, but that's not what this is, and it's time I set him straight. "I didn't want to say anything in front of my wife earlier," I begin, sounding slightly breathless, "but Jess isn't missing. She texted me this morning."

Price raises his brows, inviting me to continue.

"I know what you're thinking, but we're not having an affair," I hasten to add. "It's just that I couldn't say much because my wife already suspects Jess of being behind everything that's happening. I promised I'd break off all contact with her. If Lexi finds out we're still communicating, things could get awkward. She's in a fragile enough state after the attack in the park, and the miscarriage, and all the other stuff that's been going on."

Price blinks at me, expressionless.

I feel the pressure to keep talking but I resist, holding his gaze in return.

He rests his elbows on the desk. "What was this text from Jess about?"

I wish she would disappear off the face of the earth. I swallow the lump in my throat. "She, uh, she said she wished things could have been different between us."

"Different how?"

I shrug. "I think she regrets breaking up. But we both know that ship has sailed." I lean forward in my chair. "I'm committed to my wife, Officer Price. Jess and I were good friends before we started dating—she's always been easy to talk to. I needed someone to bounce things off. Lexi ... she's a basket case right now." I break off abruptly, realizing too late that I shouldn't have said that about my wife. It's the kind of thing that could come back to haunt me.

Price rubs a finger across the tip of his nose as he jots down a few notes. "Naomi said you met up with Jess last night." He looks pointedly at me.

I shake my head. "I asked her to meet me. I ... just wanted to make sure she wasn't behind the harassment. But we never did get together. She didn't text me back until this morning."

Price clears his throat. I'm beginning to recognize a pattern. Clearing his throat is how he underlines things he deems important. "You realize how this looks, don't you? You accused your ex-girlfriend of harassing your wife, then you asked her to meet you, and now she's disappeared."

"She hasn't disappeared! I told you, she texted me this morning."

"Can I take a look at the text?"

I shift in my seat. "I already told you what it was about."

Price flattens his lips. "If you prefer, I could get a warrant."

"Seriously?"

His eyes bore into me. "A young woman didn't come home last night. Is that serious enough for you?"

My shoulders slump when I realize there's no way around this. Sooner or later, Price will see that text and when he does, Jess will become the prime suspect in the attack on Lexi. My stomach churns at the thought. I can't let that happen. I need to find Jess first.

I slide my chair out and get to my feet. "We're done here. If you have anything else to ask me, you can talk to my lawyer."

19

LEXI

On the ride home from the station, Cash doesn't have much to say about his interview with Officer Price. He tells me it was just a formality —that the police are talking to all of Jess's *acquaintances*, as he put it. He denies being the last person to see her but, as I pointed out, Naomi must have had a good reason for saying that. That's when he told me he's going to retain a lawyer.

"Just as a precaution to protect my rights," he assures me. "Price is getting a warrant for my phone. I told him he's wasting his time—Jess will probably show up again before he even gets his warrant."

"And what if she doesn't? This is serious. Did you text her anything that could be misinterpreted as threatening?"

"Of course not! I just told her to back off with the vile messages, that's all."

I dig my nails into my palms, but I don't respond. I can tell by his defensive manner that he's not coming clean with me. I suspect he's been texting Jess a whole lot more than a reprimand.

The cheap coffee I consumed at the police station curdles

in my stomach when we pull into our driveway and I remember that we still have an obnoxious house guest to contend with, on top of everything else. The only comforting thought is that the wicked witch will be banished by tomorrow.

"Where have you two been all this time?" Eleanor unloads on us, the minute we step inside the house.

"I left you a note," Cash says. "We had errands to run."

"At this time of night? What kind of errands? The refrigerator's stocked—mostly with objectionable items, I have to admit."

Cash frowns. "It's really none of your business—"

"We were at the police station, Eleanor," I cut in, with a plastic smile. "Cash's ex-girlfriend, Jess—the one you admire so much—is missing."

"Missing?" Eleanor squeezes her wrinkled lips together. "Are you sure you don't have your wires crossed, dear? You've been so absentminded lately."

I fold my arms in front of me, ignoring the dig. "Her sister says she never came home last night. She reported her missing to the police."

Eleanor reaches for the back of a chair and sinks into it. "Oh my, that is ... concerning. Do the police have any leads?"

I throw Cash an irked look. "Other than your son, no."

Eleanor's eyes spring wide. "What's that supposed to mean?"

I shrug. "According to Naomi, Cash was the last person to see her."

Eleanor flaps her hand in protest. "I don't believe that little tramp for a minute. She's still incensed at Cash for breaking up with her sister. I never did care for her snarky attitude."

Cash's phone chimes with an incoming message.

"It's Naomi," he says, his voice unexpectedly upbeat. "She just got a text from Jess."

Eleanor lets out a disparaging snort. "Typical! Much ado about nothing. Any excuse to drag my son through the mud. I knew it was premature to report her missing."

Cash runs his fingers through his hair. "It was an odd text, though. Jess said she was going away for a few weeks. She told Naomi she'll be traveling so she won't be in touch much."

"That's convenient," I say. "The police want to talk to her, and she suddenly takes off on an extended trip." I narrow my eyes at Cash. "Is that why you met up with her—to warn her?"

"Don't be like that, Lexi—"

"Like what?" I snap. "A wife who knows she's being played for a fool, who's had enough of her husband running around with his ex behind her back?"

Eleanor begins to cluck in the background. "I tried to warn you, Cash. She's far too temperamental to be the mother of your children."

I reach for the pack of smiley face notecards in my pocket and toss them onto the table where they spin to a stop in front of her. "Apparently, I'm not the unhinged one. You've been getting off on taunting me with sick messages: *I'm watching you!* Sound familiar?"

"What in the world are you talking about now?" Eleanor asks, cocking her head to one side, and looking at me as if I'm cognitively impaired.

"We found these in your house. They match the card that was sent to me."

"You were in my house? How dare—"

"I had to meet with the contractor," Cash lies, in a vain

attempt to smooth things over. He's wasting his time. I'm just getting started.

"What else have you done to intimidate me?" I demand. "Did you pay someone to spray paint my house?"

Eleanor widens her eyes in mock outrage. "Have you completely lost your mind? Cash, say something! Do you hear what she's accusing me of?"

"I can't do this anymore," he growls, before turning and stomping out of the room.

I stand there, shaking, as he slams the door behind him. How dare he walk out of the room when he should be speaking out in my defense!

Eleanor gives a patronizing shake of her head. "See what you've done now? You and your wild accusations! You're a dismal excuse for a wife. Cash would have been better off if he'd married Jess. If you'd massaged the situation a little, this could all have turned out differently."

"*Massaged*?" I spit the word out as I stomp over to the door. "Maybe if you'd massaged his ego less, he wouldn't have thought he could string two women along all this time!"

I make a point of slamming the door even more loudly than Cash did, before sweeping into the family room to confront him. He's sprawled out on the couch, one hand shielding his eyes. I stand over him and nudge him. "You can't run away from me like that—I'm your wife and I deserve to know what's going on."

Cash blinks at me in a defeated fashion. "I wish I knew. I'm so sorry, Lexi. I had no idea Jess would turn on me like this. I confronted her about harassing you and she got really angry. She must have panicked and disappeared when she realized the police wanted to talk to her. I swear to you there's nothing going on between us. As far as I'm concerned, I hope she keeps traveling forever. I never want to hear from her again."

I blow out a heavy breath and sink down on the edge of the couch. He sounds genuinely contrite—maybe he's finally seen Jess's true colors. "The good thing is if she's gone, we don't have to live in dread of what's going to happen next," I say, twisting my lips. "Other than whatever petty pranks your mother continues to play."

Cash reaches for my hand and rubs his thumb slowly back-and-forth over my knuckles. "I still can't believe she sent that sick card. Scratch that. I *can* believe she sent it—I should have listened to you. It's even possible she egged Jess on, put her up to pulling all those awful stunts." He sits upright and pulls his phone out of his back pocket. "I'm going to text Tom and ask if I can drop Mom off at his place this afternoon instead of tomorrow. No point in her even unpacking at our place. I'm sick of her games. I should never have let her walk all over you like I did."

I rest my head on Cash's shoulder, listening as he makes the necessary arrangements with Tom. A sense of serenity envelops me when he hangs up. Finally, we can look forward to a little peace in our own home.

When Cash returns later on that evening after dropping Eleanor off, we put on an action movie and snuggle up in bed sipping cabernet and eating chocolate covered almonds. We're engrossed in a high velocity chase scene when Cash's phone chirps beneath the covers.

He fishes it out and we stare at the message on the screen in disbelief: *I'm never far away. My favorite thing is watching you through the window. J*

20

LEXI

I scream, instinctively pulling the covers up to my chin as though Jess is here in the room with us. Cash leaps out of bed and dashes across the floor to the window. He looks this way and that, but it's dark outside—impossible to spot a shadowy figure beating a hasty retreat. He yanks the curtains closed and returns to bed, a smoldering look in his eyes. "She's not out there. She's just toying with us."

"You don't know that. She's been inside the house before. Are you sure you locked the front door when you came back from dropping your mother off?"

He nods. "I'm positive."

"And the back door?"

"Yes."

"She signed it this time," I say quietly. "*J for Jess.* She wants us to know it's her. And she's using another new number. She's never going to stop."

Cash scowls. "Then we'll just have to stop her. I'll change my phone number first thing tomorrow." He wraps a muscular arm around my shoulder and pulls me tight to his chest. "I'm going to make this up to you. How about we go away this weekend? You said you wanted to get out of here, and I promised you we'd talk about it. We can make it happen for a couple of days, at least."

I give a tentative nod. "I'd like that very much. No phones, no exes, no mother-in-law!"

Cash kisses me on the forehead. "I'll make all the arrangements. You won't have to do a thing, other than pack a bag."

CASH TAKES Friday afternoon off so we can leave early for our weekend getaway. It's only a forty-five-minute drive to the inn we're staying at, in a beautiful quaint little seaside village called Driftwood Bay which we both love. It's also only fifteen minutes from Anya's house, so we can pick Mila up on our way back on Sunday night as it's Cash's week to have her.

I haven't spoken a word to Eleanor since our latest blowup. She was outraged when Cash insisted on taking her over to Tom's a day early, but Cash was equally incensed with her for denying she sent me that dumb, smiley-face card. In the end, Eleanor yelled at him that I deserved everything I got and slammed the door of Tom's apartment in his face. She's going to end up bitter and lonely, without even her son in her life, but she's brought it on herself. I don't have much sympathy for her. I intend to put her and her miserable existence out of my mind for the next two days.

"What do you want to do this weekend?" Cash asks, after we check in to our room at The Seashell Inn.

I give him a mischievous grin. "How about we rent one of those four-wheeled pedal bikes with the canopies and ride around town like we're real tourists?"

"Nope. I can promise you that's not going to happen. Next."

"Fine. If you won't ride around town with me, then I'll drag you into every last nicknack shop I can find."

Cash grins sheepishly. "I deserve it. Just so long as I get a double scoop waffle cone for my trouble."

"Deal! Where do you want to eat tonight?"

"How about Fisherman's Grill? I'm craving some of their Cajun Sea Bass."

"That place is popular. We'd better call and make a reservation."

Cash dials their number and manages to snag a table for 5:30 P.M. It's early but we can go for a walk along the beach afterward. It will be nice to spend some time alone with my husband in a peaceful environment. There's been so much craziness going on in our lives lately, and last weekend he was in Vegas, so we've barely had a minute to connect.

As if reading my thoughts, Cash comes up behind me and kneads my shoulders. "Exactly what the doctor ordered, just the two of us enjoying a little down time and each other's company."

I roll my shoulders and smile, not wanting to spoil the moment by bringing up any of the unpleasantness we will inevitably have to talk about at some point over the course of the weekend—beginning with setting some boundaries with Eleanor. I'm not prepared to put up with any more of her abusive behavior. And after her latest stunt, Cash is firmly on my side.

Dinner is melt-in-your-mouth-magical, and Cash does his very best to make me feel loved. We even talk about trying again for another child, which is a good indication he's fully committed to our relationship. Maybe now that Jess has revealed her true nature, he's finally ready to let her go, emotionally as well as physically. She hasn't won, after all.

We split a molten chocolate lava cake for dessert, then head to the strand to walk off the calories.

"This is the happiest I've been in weeks," I say, clasping Cash's hand tightly, as I dangle my leather sandals from my fingers.

"And the most relaxed," he adds with a contented sigh.

"That's because we're away from Creek Falls. I really don't want to live there anymore. That place has too many bad memories—for both of us: Anya's affair, everything Jess has done to destroy our relationship, losing our baby, your mother hovering over us like a fiendish specter." I shiver despite the warmth of the evening. "Not to mention the stabbing—I could have been killed."

Cash sighs. "It's not as easy as packing up and moving on. I have Mila to think about."

"We don't have to move out of state, just a different town, a new house—one that isn't filled with memories of your ex-wife. We need a fresh start."

"How about Driftwood Bay?" Cash asks. "I could get used to this leisurely pace."

I laugh. "Not unless you're content to sell ice cream in waffle cones for a living. This place isn't exactly an engineering hub."

"Tell you what," Cash says, tugging me closer. "How about we do some research and visit a few places over the next couple of months—kick start the process?"

I nestle my head contentedly against his shoulder. "It's a step in the right direction. That's all I'm asking for."

. . .

I WAKE with a jolt the following morning to the sound of my phone ringing. Cash groans in my ear. "What time is it?"

"Eight-thirty," I say, stifling a yawn.

"Ugh, I wish you'd turn your phone off at night."

"Sorry, I forgot," I mumble, as I reach for it on the bedside cabinet. "It's Helen, next door. I'd better take this. She might have fallen or something. Knowing Wade, he's passed out on his couch, oblivious."

I hit the speaker button. "Good morning, Helen!"

"Hello, Lexi, dear. Are you home?"

"No. Cash and I are out of town for a couple of days."

"Oh, I see," Helen answers, sounding flustered. "I suppose you have someone managing the garage sale, in that case."

I shoot Cash a bewildered look. He sits up on one elbow, frowning.

"What garage sale, Helen?"

"Well, I'm looking out my front window right now and your garage door is wide open and there are people—strangers—milling around and walking off with stuff. My eyesight's not the best, of course, but for the life of me I can't see who's collecting the money."

"What kind of stuff are they walking away with?" I ask in a measured tone, my eyes locked on Cash.

"All sorts of things: golf clubs, a baby stroller, tools. I think I see a man with a motorcycle helmet under his arm, although I don't have my glasses on so I can't say for sure if that's what I'm looking at."

Cash throws back the covers and springs from the bed. "Hang up and call the police!"

21

LEXI

Ten minutes later, we're wheeling out of The Seashell Inn parking lot, heading for home.

"If this is Jess's idea of dark humor, I'm going to kill her," Cash growls, tugging at his seatbelt.

"Surely she wouldn't dare show her face anywhere near our house right now," I say, gripping the edge of my seat as we hurtle along the winding road leading back to the highway.

"She doesn't have to. She could have paid someone else to run a bogus garage sale." Cash rubs a hand over his unshaven jaw. "What did the police say?"

"They're going to send someone to the house to put a stop to it. I told them we hadn't authorized a garage sale, and we knew nothing about it until one of our neighbors called us."

"I texted Tom, too, asked if he could go over there and sort it out, but he's out of town. What I want to know is how on earth Jess knew we'd be gone this weekend," Cash says, tapping the steering wheel angrily.

"Good question. The only people who knew we were

leaving town were your mother, and Anya, of course, when we told her we'd pick Mila up on our way back." I stare fixedly through the windscreen. "I thought all along your mother might have been scheming with Jess. This confirms it, as far as I'm concerned. She knew we were gone, and she saw an opportunity to take revenge on us for kicking her out of the house."

Cash says nothing but his jaw is set like cement. He's had about all he can take. Maybe this will be enough to persuade him to move away from Creek Falls for good.

HELEN IS STANDING in our driveway talking to the police when we arrive back at the house. They've already put a halt to the proceedings, but not before we lost a considerable number of valuable items, including a tub of brand-new baby clothes. Tossed to one side of the driveway is a large cardboard sign with the words: FREE *items to good homes. Pickup only. Everything must go!*

"No wonder the place was swarming with people," Cash fumes.

"There was no one supervising things when we arrived on the scene. Any idea who was behind this?" a young police officer with butch arms and gleaming white teeth asks.

"I know exactly who was behind it," Cash shoots back. "I can give you a name and a phone number, but I guarantee you won't find her. She's disappeared— she told her family she would be traveling for the next few weeks. She's potentially facing a host of charges, including attempted murder. Officer Price is handling our case. He'll fill you in on what's been going on."

The police officer paints a bleak picture when it comes

to the prospect of retrieving our stolen goods, but we go through our garage and provide them with a detailed description of everything we can think of that's missing, nonetheless. Practically all the baby gear is gone: car seat, swing, stroller. Hot ticket items, no doubt—they were all brand new. By the time we're done, I'm bawling my eyes out. Helen shuffle walks me over to her house to fix me some tea and a slice of freshly baked banana walnut loaf while Cash finishes up with the police.

"There you go, dear," Helen says, setting a tray down on the table between us. I sip the hot tea gratefully, hugging the mug in my hands. "Thank you. This is exactly what I needed. I can't stop shivering. I feel so violated."

"It's a shocking thing to happen in a neighborhood like this," Helen agrees. "I called you as soon as I realized what was going on. I saw you two drive off yesterday, so I didn't think you were home. It struck me as odd that you would have a garage sale while you were gone."

"Thank goodness you called, or we might have lost a whole lot more than we did." I break off a piece of loaf and put it in my mouth. "Mmm! This is delicious. I need the recipe."

Helen peers at me over her readers. "I overheard Cash talking to the police. Do you really think his ex-girlfriend was behind it?"

And his mother, I'm tempted to add. I hesitate before giving a doleful nod. "It looks that way. Cash finally admitted to me that he'd stayed in touch with Jess—just as friends—but he realizes now it might have been a mistake. She's become increasingly jealous of our relationship—it intensified when I became pregnant. Cash was a bit naive about the whole situation, at first."

Helen smooths a sparrow-like hand over her skirt,

blinking at me. "How did Jess get into your garage—I assume it was locked?"

"I don't know. Unless ..."

"Unless?" Helen prompts.

"Unless Eleanor gave her the code."

Helen sits back and raises her mug to her lips. She's about to take a sip when she suddenly sets it back down with a thunk. "Could Cash have given it to her?"

I throw her a startled look. "He wouldn't have done that. He knows Jess has been harassing us—at least, he suspects as much."

"Maybe you're the one who's being naive, dear." Helen leans back in her chair. "And I know what you're thinking: *who are you to be talking, Helen, allowing your pot-smoking son to sponge off you like you do.* But it's hard when you get older, and you can't make the choices you want to make. I'd rather live here in my own home than in a facility, and I can't manage without Wade's help—unreliable as he is. You, on the other hand, have choices. You don't have to let a man dictate the terms of your life."

I frown down at the lemon slice floating on top of my tea before raising my head and meeting her gaze. "Do you ... know something, Helen? Have you seen anything, by chance?"

"Nothing concrete, dear. But I have my suspicions, and enough sense to know not to trust a man who lies to you."

A deep-throated laugh fills the room as Wade barges in. "Or a husband who hangs out at The Black Horse Tavern with his sexy ex."

22

CASH

"I've asked Anya to keep Mila next week, too," I tell Lexi, after the police leave. "It's not safe for her to stay here with everything that's going on. Anya's already freaked out enough about the fire at my mom's. Next, she'll be threatening to sue me for full custody."

Lexi nods distractedly. "That's fine. Probably for the best."

I pour myself a glass of water and join her on the couch. "I checked the camera on the east gable, and it shows a hooded figure in baggy clothes opening up the garage around three this morning. The police took a look at the footage, but unless we can identify the person, they say there's not much they can do."

Lexi picks at a hangnail and doesn't respond.

I pull her to me. "Hey, are you okay?"

"No, of course I'm not okay! They took all the baby gear, even the clothes."

"It's just stuff, honey. Don't worry, we'll get more when we need it. Is that all that's bothering you?"

She shrugs. "Wade said something when I was over at Helen's."

"What?" I narrow my eyes, trying to read her expression. "Did he see something?"

After a long pause, she shakes her head in a dismissive manner. "He thought he saw a couple who looked familiar. He was probably mistaken. You know him. He's in his own world half the time."

"But what if it's important?" I counter, rifling a hand through my hair. "We should have him talk to the police—he might be able to give them a description. Were they casing the place? Does he know their names?"

Lexi looks at me strangely, then shakes her head. "No. He wasn't very helpful. He had no details."

I rub a hand over my jaw, deflating a little. For a moment, I was hopeful we might have had a witness. But I should have known better. Wade was likely just spouting off —trying to inject himself into the situation.

"This is the second time someone's been in our house," I say. "We're going to have to take some drastic measures to make sure we're safe going forward."

"What kind of measures?" Lexi asks, sounding wary.

"We need to change both of our phone numbers, for starters."

"Why mine? It's you she's texting."

"She texted you as well: *ignoring me makes me angrier.* Remember? And if I change my number, she may turn all her fury on you. We need a fresh start, like you keep saying."

Lexi hugs her arms around herself—a protective gesture that makes me feel less of a man for exposing her to this nightmare to begin with. I deeply regret messaging with Jess behind her back. It was inexcusable. The least I can do now is double my efforts to make sure Lexi feels safe going forward. I'll call Verizon first chance I get and sort out new numbers for both of us.

I take a deep breath before divulging the next part of my plan—the part I suspect might meet with some resistance. "I've decided to buy a gun for protection. Jess—if it is her—has already proven she's willing to stop at nothing to take you out. Just because her first attempt in the park failed, it doesn't mean she won't try again."

Lexi recoils in horror. "You know how I feel about guns." She picks nervously at her fingers waiting for me to respond.

I reach for her hand and fold it into mine. "This isn't about feelings anymore. We aren't dealing with some hypothetical situation. My crazy ex is trying to kill you. I feel partly responsible for causing this nightmare, and I need to take control of it. I've been thinking about buying a gun ever since you were attacked in the park. I've already completed the background check."

The doorbell rings and I grab Lexi, who's halfway out of her seat. "Stay here. I'll get it." Maybe I'm being overprotective but I'm not willing to risk exposing her to any more danger today.

When I open the front door and see my mother standing on the steps, I'm doubly relieved I made Lexi sit back down.

"Tom told me what happened. My poor boy!" Mom exclaims, trying to hand me a plate of freshly baked muffins which I studiously ignore despite the tantalizing smell of brown butter sugar wafting through the air. "Have you calculated your losses yet? Homeowner's insurance will cover it. You're not hurt, are you?" Her eyes travel expertly over me.

"I'm fine; Lexi's fine too. Thanks for asking," I reply stiffly.

Mom arches a thin brow at me. "Aren't you going to invite me in? I drove all the way over here as soon as I heard."

"We didn't invite you. Boundaries, remember?" I fold my arms across my chest and lean against the doorpost, blocking the doorway. "Did you give Jess the code to our garage?"

"Really, Cash!" she responds, sounding scandalized. "Did that little vixen Lexi put you up to this? You ought to be ashamed of yourself accusing your own mother of—"

"*Did* you, Mom?"

She blinks at me, the platter of muffins twitching in her hand. "I don't recall giving it to her. But it's possible I did, at some point. I mean she was your girlfriend, after all."

"*Was*, as in past tense."

"Yes, well, I always harbored hope you would marry that girl—she's smart as a whip."

"Apparently," I grumble. "By the sound of things, she's got you under her spell."

Mom's pale, wrinkled lips curl slowly upward. "You're completely smitten with her, still. You would do anything for Jessica—lie, cheat or steal."

I follow my mother's gaze over my left shoulder to see Lexi standing in the hall a few feet behind me.

Judging by the look on her face, she's been listening to every word—a fact my mother was only too well aware of.

23

CASH

I take a step back to place a protective arm around Lexi's shoulders and glare at my mother. "It's time you left," I say, through gritted teeth.

She sets the platter of muffins on the console table just inside the door, a wounded expression on her face. "Lexi, dear, these are for you. An olive branch of sorts. Upon reflection, I realize I was a little sharp with you the last time we conversed."

Lexi stares back at her, expressionless.

I slam the door closed before Mom can say another word, then hug Lexi. "I'm so sorry," I say, stroking her hair. "I wouldn't have opened the door if I'd known it was her. I thought it might have been Price. I left him a message earlier about the phony garage sale."

"I can't believe your mom apologized to me, not that it sounded in any way sincere. I know she blames me for kicking her out of our house." Lexi eyes the muffins warily. "Those are probably laced with arsenic. They do smell good though."

I give her a rueful grin. "I doubt my mother would risk

poisoning her only son. They're just her lame attempt to get back into our good graces. Don't worry, it's not going to work."

"So you don't think the muffins will explode in our faces, or leave us salivating cyanide?" Lexi asks with a nervous giggle.

"The odds are in our favor," I assure her.

Lexi tweaks a small smile. "Go for it! I'll pass."

I WAS wrong about the muffins. Thirty minutes later, I'm wrestling with the most awful stomach cramps and throwing up violently. At least Lexi had the good sense not to touch them. Seems I've underestimated my own mother's capacity for revenge.

When the nausea finally subsides, I call her up and chew her out.

"Don't be ridiculous, Cash," she purrs. "What do you take me for? You probably picked up a stomach bug somewhere."

"I didn't pick up anything other than your contaminated muffins. I ate two and started throwing up almost immediately afterward. Lexi didn't touch them and she's fine. If this is your idea of getting back at her because she made you leave, you're even sicker than I realized!"

"I don't know what to tell you, Cash, darling. I absolutely did not put anything in those muffins."

"Right! Just like you absolutely did not send Lexi that vile card!"

"That's nons—"

I end the call before she can finish her sentence. I'm too exhausted from retching to continue arguing with her. She's never going to admit to any wrongdoing.

Lexi comes back into the room with a wet rag for my forehead. "Feeling any better?"

"A little. My stomach's finally beginning to settle now that I've gotten rid of the contents. Of course, Mom denies putting anything in the muffins."

"I tossed the rest of them," Lexi says. "Better safe than sorry."

"Good," I say, then catch myself. "Wait! On second thoughts, let's save them! Maybe I'll have them tested."

Lexi's eyes grow wide. "Why? Are you going to try and have her prosecuted?"

"No. Whatever she put in the muffins wasn't poisonous. She wasn't trying to kill you, just make you feel miserable. I bet she doctored them to get back at you for kicking her out. This is the end of the road for our relationship. As far as I'm concerned, I couldn't care less if I never set eyes on my mother again."

Lexi looks pensive. "I told you she was spiteful. You didn't believe me. You kept making excuses for her behavior."

"I believe you now." I groan, struggling to my feet. "Where were we before she showed up at the door?"

A flicker of a frown crosses Lexi's brow. "Guns and new phone numbers."

"That's right. Can you pass me my laptop?"

I spend the next couple of hours on the phone sorting out our new numbers with Verizon, and informing all our contacts, while Lexi makes a run to the store for some soup and ginger beer. When I hang up, I remember the muffins and retrieve a couple from the trash. After finding a place online that will analyze them within ten business days, I package them up as directed. Lexi still hasn't returned from the store, but I'm feeling much better, so I decide to take the package to the post office and stop by the gun store on my way back. I hate that I don't feel safe sleeping in my own house anymore. Lexi's right. We need to find someplace new and start over. Until then, I'll do everything in my power to defend my wife and daughter.

On the way to the gun store, I call Anya and ask to speak to Mila.

"Hi Daddy!" she squeals into the phone in her shrill, little voice.

"Hi baby! How was school?"

"Good. 'Cept Tommy spitted at me on the playground."

"Make sure you tell him boys who spit won't be able to run fast when they grow up. That oughta make him stop."

"You're silly, Daddy!" Mila chuckles.

"What are you up to now?" I ask.

"Nothing. Mommy's mad so she won't play with me."

Grimacing, I pull into the strip mall parking lot outside the gun store and switch off the ignition. "Why's she mad?"

Mila lets out a dramatic sigh. "'Cause you and Lexi don't want me, so she has to have me *all* the time, and she says it's not fair."

A stabbing pain hits me in the gut. "That's not true, honey. Lexi and I love you very much. It's just that things have been—" I almost say *dangerous* but I don't want to scare my daughter. "Things have been difficult at our house lately. Lexi's been through a lot."

"Yup," Mila agrees. "Mommy says things are going to get a lot more bad for that cow."

24

LEXI

I push my cart up and down the grocery aisles in a daze, stopping every now and then to pick up an item and stare at the label in an effort to blend in with the other shoppers. I can't concentrate on what I'm doing because I'm too busy thinking about everything that's happened in the past few hours. I can't get what Wade said about seeing Cash and Jess at the Black Horse Tavern out of my mind. At least, I assume it was Jess. Could it have been Anya? I can't imagine her wanting anything to do with him —it must have been Jess. I can't deny any longer that my husband is a liar. It sickens me to think he hasn't just been texting Jess this whole time. It's worse. He's been meeting up with her, going for drinks with her—who knows what else? Helen's warning not to trust a man who lies circles on a loop inside my head.

Wade made it sound as if it wasn't a one-time occurrence, although when I questioned him, he couldn't give me specific dates or times. I'll have to ask him more about it when Helen isn't around. She already has her antenna up when it comes to Cash, and I don't want her relaying her suspicions to the police.

Cash is such a great guy when I have his full attention, but now I see that he's weak. Unable to resist Jess's charms. And she *is* charming, gregarious, intelligent, kind-hearted, and all sorts of other admirable polysyllabic words Cash has used to describe her in the past. As has Eleanor—far too frequently for my liking. It's as though they like to rub it in. My predecessors continue to haunt me, despite how hard I try to be the perfect wife and daughter-in-law.

Tears prickle and I battle to keep from breaking down in the canned goods aisle. All I can think about is Cash and Jess in the tavern, drinking and laughing together, sharing private jokes and memories—maybe a stolen kiss or two. I won't let Jess do this to me. Even with Eleanor's backing, she won't win. I'm not going to roll over and give up my husband without a fight. With renewed resolve, I ram the shopping cart into motion, trying to remember what I came in here for. Soup and crackers? Soup and something or other.

By the time I get back to the house, I've managed to get my emotions back under control. After giving it some thought, I decide not to confront Cash about what Wade said. It's not that I don't believe Wade. It's just that he's a hopelessly unreliable witness. He couldn't give me a description of the woman Cash was with, and he went back-and-forth about how many times he'd seen them together in the tavern. If I confront Cash with inaccurate information, it will be too easy for him to talk his way out of it.

When I arrive back at the house, I'm shocked to see Eleanor's car in the driveway. What is she doing here? Didn't she get the memo that she's not welcome in our home anymore? I park along the curb and walk up to her car, but she's not in it. My stomach twists. She must be inside with

Cash. She probably brought him some of her *famous*—because what else would it be?—homemade chicken noodle soup to ingratiate herself with him. My sub-par canned soup offering won't be able to compete. I stand on the front step and take a deep breath, forcing myself to appear calm as I prepare to greet them.

Eleanor is sitting alone at the kitchen table when I walk in. She looks up, disappointment flooding her face when she catches sight of me. "Oh, it's … you. Where's Cash?"

I frown, unloading the groceries onto the counter. "He's not here?"

Eleanor tuts at my ignorance. "You don't know where your sick husband is? I can't believe you left him alone when he was so violently ill. His car's not in the garage. What if he had to drive himself to the hospital?"

I bristle at her condescending tone. "He threw up a few times. That was the height of it. I doubt he's at the ER. If you must know, I went to get him some soup."

Eleanor raises her brows appraisingly. "A good wife would *make* her husband some soup, not purchase it in a can." She lets out a long-suffering sigh. "However, you needn't trouble yourself. I brought his favorite. It's a recipe of mine he's enjoyed since childhood." She gives a bitter laugh. "I imagine he's barely had time to familiarize himself with your recipes in all of the eight—or are we up to nine? —months he's known you."

I scrunch the empty grocery bag into a ball with my fist. "Either you leave now or I'm calling the police."

"You really do have the most appalling manners." Eleanor stands and reaches for her sensible black purse on the table. "I put Cash's soup on the top shelf in the fridge. There's a post-it note taped to it with bulleted instructions on how to reheat it. I trust you'll be able to follow them."

With that, she marches out the front door without as much as a perfunctory goodbye.

The minute she drives off, I remove the tub of chicken noodle soup from the fridge and dump it down the garbage disposal. I watch it swirling to its death with satisfaction, then put a pot on the stove to heat up the can of soup I bought at the store.

Another twenty minutes go by before I hear Cash's car pull into the garage. "Why are you parked at the curb?" he asks, tromping into the kitchen.

I stare pointedly at the box he sets on the counter. He actually did it—he bought a gun. A small shiver goes through me. "Your mother was here. Checking up on you. Being her usual delightful self."

His expression darkens. "You shouldn't have invited her in."

"I didn't. She let herself in. She was sitting at the kitchen table when I got back from the store. I told her to leave, or I'd call the police." I fold my arms and frown. "Makes me wonder if she let herself into the garage, too."

Cash shakes his head. "That garage sale stunt wasn't her doing. She would never have given away the expensive golf clubs she bought me." He reaches for the box on the counter and removes the handgun, placing it carefully on the table in front of me. "I'm going to show you how to use this."

I give an adamant shake of my head. "I don't want to know. I could never shoot someone."

Cash places a hand on my belly. "What if you get pregnant again? Wouldn't you do whatever you had to do to protect our baby?"

I swallow hard. After a long moment, I give a tentative nod. "Okay."

"I don't like this any more than you do, but we don't have a choice," Cash says.

He proceeds to demonstrate the safety lock, how to load and unload the handgun, and then makes me do it several times until he's satisfied I can manage it seamlessly.

"I picked up a small wall safe for our bedroom too," he says. "That way, if anyone breaks in at night, we'll be able to access the gun before they come upstairs."

He fetches the safe from the car and, after going back-and-forth for several minutes on a passcode, we finally agree on our anniversary. "It's not the best idea," Cash admits. "But it needs to be a number we can both remember under pressure. Anya and I used Mila's birthday for almost everything and we've never been the victims of identity theft."

"Works for me," I say.

Cash hefts the safe into his arms. "Okay, let's go upstairs and find a good spot for this."

I follow him up to our bedroom, stopping dead in my tracks in the doorway. The closet door is ajar, the gutted remains of my wedding dress spilling out like confetti.

Officer Price takes a sip of the coffee Cash made for him before pulling out his notebook. "What time did you arrive back from the store, Lexi?" he begins.

I furrow my brow, trying to remember. My mind was so scattered after discovering my mother-in-law in my kitchen that I didn't pay any attention to the time.

"I was gone longer than I intended," I say. "It must have been close to four o'clock. Like I said, Eleanor was already in the house, sitting at my kitchen table."

"I can tell you exactly what time they both arrived," Cash offers, pulling out his phone. He taps on the camera app and scrolls through until he finds the timestamp he's looking for. "Here we go. Lexi got home at 3:49 P.M. My mother went into the house at 3:26 P.M."

Price makes a note of the times, then sets down his pen. He leans his elbows on the table and interlocks his fingers, preparing to address us like a doctor delivering an unfavorable report. "The long and the short of it is, I can have your mother arrested for trespassing and vandalism, if that's how you'd like to proceed. It's up to you if you want to try and handle this within the family or turn it into a police matter."

I glance uncertainly at Cash. I know what I want to do, but this has got to be his decision. He already called his mother before Price got here and chewed her out for destroying my wedding dress, but she denied it, like she always does. Cash told me she wasn't in the least remorseful, even tried to blame it on me and my carelessness. He warned her he'd bought a gun and wouldn't hesitate to use it if we caught anyone trespassing on our property again. She was appalled, of course, and told him I was too unstable to be around weapons.

"I want to press charges," Cash says, at length. His face falls as the words leave his lips. This is unbearably hard for him, but motherly bond or not, Eleanor has gone too far this time.

"Fair enough." Price picks up his pen and jots something down on his notepad.

"It's not just the wedding dress," Cash explains. "Earlier this morning, she dropped off some muffins she'd made for Lexi. I ate a couple of them, and they made me violently ill. She was mad at us for kicking her out of the house—she blamed it on Lexi—and I think it was her way of getting back at her. Now that I think about it, she probably threw the bleach over Lexi's maternity clothes too. She accused her of deliberately getting pregnant to trap me."

"No. That couldn't have been her," I interrupt. "We were at your mom's that evening, remember? It must have been Jess."

"We think they're working together," Cash says grimly.

Price drums his fingers on the table, moving his jowls back and forth in an off-putting manner. I don't think he's ruled out Cash as a suspect in Jess's disappearance yet, despite mounting evidence that she's alive and well and bent on harassing us at every turn.

"Do you think your mother might know where Jess is?" Price asks.

Cash scratches the stubble on his chin as he considers the question. "It wouldn't surprise me if she does. She might even be hiding her."

Price snaps his notebook shut and slips it into his pocket before rising from the table. "I'll bring her in for questioning. We'll book her and release her. Given your history with her, it might be advisable to keep your doors and windows locked."

Cash gives a somber nod. "Believe me, we're taking every possible precaution."

I shift uncomfortably in my chair, trying not to look over at the counter where he left the empty handgun box. Cash would never shoot his mother, would he? As if reading my thoughts, Price's keen gaze locks with mine. He gives me a measured nod as Cash escorts him to the door. I'm not sure what it was meant to convey, or if he's even on our side.

Sinking farther down in my chair, I exhale loudly, relieved to see the back of Officer Price. I haven't warmed up to him over the course of the investigation, and I'm pretty sure the feeling's mutual. What's worse is that I'm convinced he's not very good at his job. If he was, he'd have found Jess and arrested her by now. Instead, he's still wasting time trying to procure a warrant for Cash's phone, with no probable cause to think he knows anything whatsoever about Jess's disappearance.

"Right, that's it," Cash announces, striding back into the kitchen. "We're jumping on Zillow this very minute. We need to get out of here before something else happens. I hate this house now as much as you do." He grabs his laptop from the counter and sits down next to me. "Help me out with the specs. No more than an hour's drive from here, minimum three-bedroom—preferably with a pool for Mila. Two-story. I don't think I'll ever feel safe sleeping on the ground floor again after this."

I pull my chair a little closer and try to concentrate, despite the myriad thoughts flitting through my brain. Is he really committing to leaving Jess behind, once and for all? A flicker of hope rises up inside me at the thought—not to mention the prospect of seeing considerably less of Eleanor.

We spend the remainder of the evening perusing various websites, compiling a list of possible houses, and discussing plans to uproot our lives and start over.

By the time we tumble into bed, I'm feeling a whole lot better about our future. With a little distance between us and the memories of Cash's past, our relationship can only grow stronger.

And with temptation out of the way, Cash will have no reason to lie to me anymore.

26

CASH

I realize now what I should have seen weeks ago—what Lexi's been trying to tell me all along. Jess and my mother are collaborating to get rid of her, and it appears they've dragged Anya into their insidious plan too. Mila's ominous warning, *things are going to get a lot more bad for that cow*, cinched it for me. Anya's relationship with Anton is on the rocks, and she's become resentful of the money I'm pouring into a new marriage and a future family —money she thinks should be earmarked for Mila.

No doubt, she was only too willing to participate in a plan to oust Lexi. My manipulative mother always gets what she wants in the end. Jess's ambition has always secured her what she wants too. And Anya's insatiable lust for money continues to drive her to stop at nothing to get what she's after. Together, the three of them are an axis of evil, and they're closing in.

In her messages, Jess as good as admits she regrets her decision to let me go, and my mother is evidently taking full advantage of the situation, egging her on to scare Lexi off. No one was ever good enough for me in my mother's eyes, but Jess, with her doctorate degree in sight, is infinitely preferable to Lexi with her paltry retail job.

Mom hasn't spoken to me since she was booked and released for trespassing and vandalism. I'm sure it's because her lawyer advised her not to have any contact with me, and not because she's finally exercising some restraint and respecting our boundaries. I can only imagine the look of shock on her perfectly powdered face when Price showed up at the door to cuff her.

What's baffling to me is that her arrest has done nothing to slow Jess down. If anything, it only seems to have incensed her. I've gotten several vitriolic emails from her over the past few days, all using different email addresses— variations of her name, mostly. The most troubling one was titled: *Be Prepared*. It was a fake obituary for Lexi with a gory attachment of a bludgeoned body. The obituary date is tomorrow. I immediately forwarded it to Price who advised me to treat it as a legitimate threat. It shook Lexi to the core, and she's agreed to stay home from work tomorrow, as a precaution.

Just this morning, on the way into the office, I received another disturbing text: *I'm drawn to you like a vampire to blood. Yours forever, J.* I tried calling the number, but it went straight to voicemail, like every other time. Somehow, Jess has got ahold of my new number. It confirms my suspicions that she and my mother are in cahoots. I deliberately excluded Jess when I notified all my contacts that I'd changed my number. In retrospect, I probably shouldn't have given the new one to my mother either. Not that it would have made any difference—Anya could have given it to both of them. Excluding her wasn't an option, with Mila's welfare to consider.

I'm still mulling over Mila's words in our last phone call. It didn't sound like something a six-year-old would make up—more like something a six-year-old might have overheard. Maybe Anya was just venting frustration over her situation. On the other hand, it might implicate her in everything that's been happening. I've always thought it was suspicious that she picked Mila up early from my mom's house the day before the fire. But why start a fire in my mother's house at all? I feel like I'm missing something, like my brain keeps misfiring.

On a whim, I pick up the phone and call Anya. If I can't get ahold of Jess, at least I can confront my ex-wife and try to figure out how deeply embroiled she is in all of this.

"I'm at work, Cash. Can't this wait?" she barks down the phone.

"Price told me you were fired from your job," I reply in an even tone.

She lets out a frustrated humph but doesn't attempt to deny it. "What do you want?"

"I need to talk to you about some alarming things Mila's been saying lately."

Anya sighs. "She's six years old. She says a lot of crazy things."

"She's been telling me about your trip to Europe. How was it?" I ask, trying a different tack.

"I don't have time for this. Why are you calling me?"

"What's going on with you, Anya?"

After another exasperated sigh, she asks, "What's that supposed to mean?"

"Mila says you and Anton were arguing a lot on the trip."

There's a beat of silence before she responds. "Since you asked, he's filed for divorce."

I scrunch my eyes closed and grip the phone a little tighter in my fist. I had a hunch their relationship was on shaky ground. To be honest, I never really thought it would last from the outset. It wasn't the first affair Anton embarked on with a married woman. He made sure Anya signed an ironclad prenup, so she stands to get nothing. Without a doubt, she's going to become my problem—again. "I'm ... sorry to hear that," I force out.

"I'm sure you are—sorry you're going to be on the hook for more money. The only reason I didn't take you back to court already is because we were well looked after as long as we were with Anton. But that free ride's over now. You can't expect me to care for Mila on the miserly sum you contribute every month."

"Is that why you said things were going to get bad for Lexi? Or should I say *that cow* as you referred to my wife?"

"Give it a break, Cash. You barely know the woman. Who proposes to a stranger after five months?"

"She was carrying my child."

"And now she's not. The only child that's your concern is Mila, and it's about time you realized it. You keep coming up with excuses for why you can't look after her. And that *stupid cow* is the reason why! She's so insanely jealous of Mila she doesn't even want her around."

"That's not true. I'm the one who made the decision that it was too dangerous for Mila to be at our house right now. Or at my mother's place either after what happened. By the way, Mom's not speaking to me at the moment, so I can't take Mila over there anymore."

"Do you blame her? You're trying to pin a bunch of trumped-up charges on her."

"They're not trumped up. She committed a series of spiteful, criminal acts directed primarily at my wife. And how do you know so much about it? Since when have you had a close relationship with my mother? You can't stand her either."

"Drastic times call for drastic measures. Anton wants me out of the house, and Eleanor has offered me a roof over my head for the foreseeable future. I guess you could say I owe her."

27

CASH

Talking to Anya has only heightened my worst fears and amped my blood pressure up another few notches. She really does have her daggers out for Lexi, and she's making no attempt to hide it. The fact that she's defending my mother after all these years of animosity between them is mind-boggling. Now that Anya's lifestyle has taken a colossal hit, she's desperate—the perfect accomplice for my mother's dirty little scheme. The troubling thing is that it's neither dirty nor little. It's deadly and large, and growing more dangerous by the day. The question burning a hole in my heart now is who the true mastermind behind it is.

I've always known my mother's propensity to be controlling and caustic, but it's gut-wrenching to think Jess could have hatched such a scheme. We were soulmates, once. But I realize now soulmates can be dangerous when they turn, like a wild animal that never truly sheds its instincts. All this time, she's been holding it against me that I gave her the ultimatum—her PhD or me. And my mother has used Jess's festering resentment to her advantage. I groan out loud when I picture Anya and Mila moving in with my mother. The last thing I want is to have to interact with her now that she's got her hooks into Anya. The crazy thing is she's never liked Anya either—she pegged her as a money-grubber from the get-go. But it seems she's willing to work with whatever dregs of humanity she's got, if it gets her what she wants.

My mind goes to the safe I installed in our bedroom closet. Despite my insistence to Lexi that we needed a gun to defend ourselves, I dread to think the day might be creeping up on me when I'm forced to use it. The fake obituary is dated tomorrow. I've managed to persuade Lexi to stay home from work, but she's made it clear she's not happy about it. She says we're playing into Jess's hands by allowing her to take control over our lives. But what choice do we have? We can't allow Jess to play out her fantasy of getting rid of Lexi and coming back into my life.

"Delivery for you," Will, my coworker, says, sticking his head through the door and tossing a package onto my desk. "Came by courier. Aren't you special?" He wiggles his brows at me and waltzes off down the corridor to the copier room, whistling a country breakup tune I can't identify but have heard a thousand times.

I reach for the package and read the shipping label. It's from a company called Settling Scores Solutions and the return address is a PO Box number. My stomach begins to churn in an all too familiar frenzy of dread. No doubt, the address is fictitious—most likely, the company, too. I can't bring myself to open it. Maybe I should bag it up and take it down to Price at the station instead, have it checked for fingerprints. I stare at the package glumly, realizing the futility of that course of action. Jess is far too clever to handle it without gloves.

I feel the padded envelope, trying to guess at its contents —too many bad movie scenes of bloody fingers coming to mind. It's relatively flat and feels soft, so I finally convince myself it contains nothing diabolical, and pluck up the courage to open it. A silky, lavender-colored scarf slithers out onto my desk. I recognize it instantly, as I lift it to my nose, inhaling the scent of her. My body floods with every kind of emotion at once—longing and rage battling for precedence inside me.

I bought this scarf for Jess the last Christmas we were together, just weeks before we parted ways. She adored it and wore it every chance she got. She even had it on when she came by the house to pick up her iPad. Why is she returning it to me now? I reach for the envelope again and peer inside. No white powder in sight. At least she's not trying to kill me with some unidentified chemical warfare agent. There's a note tucked away at the bottom. I catch it, scissor-like between my fingers, and carefully draw it out, wondering again if I should have dusted it for fingerprints first. Too late now to go back. I open the note and stare at the words in disbelief.

I want to turn myself in. Will you drive me? Meet me at our spot in the park at six this evening. Come alone.

28

CASH

I reread the note several times to make sure I've got it right. It's a stunning turn of events. Either Jess has fallen foul of my mother's agenda, or she's had a change of heart and wants to put an end to the sick campaign they've been waging. Does she genuinely want to end it? There's always a chance it could be a trap. I should probably proceed with caution, but I'm not going to be in any real danger in a public place. There are always plenty of people around at that time of day. It's not as if she'll be able to stab me and run off without anyone seeing what happened.

I want to believe she's come to her senses at last. I can't help but feel a certain measure of elation at the thought of this nightmare finally drawing to an end. The only problem will be coming up with an excuse for Lexi as to why I'm going to be late home from work this evening. I hate having to lie to her again, but I can't tell her the truth either. And I don't want to get her hopes up in case this doesn't pan out, or Jess is a no show. More important, I can't risk Lexi calling the police and scaring Jess off. It means a lot to me that she's asked me to be at her side when she turns herself in.

I rub the back of my neck, trying to pull my jumbled thoughts together. Maybe I shouldn't be flattered. After everything that's gone down, Jess electing to turn herself in seems almost too easy. I hope I'm not being naive about her true intentions.

I'm still struggling with what to tell Lexi, but as it turns out, I don't need to resort to any of the lame excuses I devised. Halfway through the afternoon, she texts me to say a co-worker has called in sick and she's been asked to cover her shift. I stare at the screen and let out a long, relieved breath, scarcely able to believe my luck. She won't have to know a thing until I call her with the good news that Jess is in police custody.

"Drinks tonight?" Will calls through the open doorway on his way back from the copier.

I fake a regretful grimace. "Sorry, can't make it. I've already got plans."

"Your loss." His gaze lands on the scarf draped across my desk. "Not your color. Missus got a birthday?"

I laugh, hastily stuffing the scarf back into the package it came in. "Something like that."

Will raises his brows with heightened interest. "So that's how it is. Don't worry, man. My lips are sealed." He swaggers off, and a ripple of worry goes through me.

Far from being sealed, Will's lips are perpetually wagging. The last thing I need is a rumor circulating among my colleagues that I'm buying gifts for someone other than my wife and having them sent to the office. I stare glumly at my computer screen. Maybe I should give the scarf to Lexi, just to cover myself. Knowing Will, he'll ask her how she liked it next time she stops by the office. Obviously, Jess doesn't want it anymore—the fact that she returned it is a signal things are finally over between us, isn't it? I sniff at it hesitantly. There's the small matter of Jess's scent still lingering on it. Lexi would know right away it had belonged to another woman. I don't know why I'm even worrying about it. This is all going to be over by this evening if Jess comes through on her promise.

The afternoon drags on, and I accomplish very little, barely managing to keep up the appearance of working when anyone walks by my office. Even now, after everything that's gone down between us, I can't deny I still have feelings for Jess. The anticipation of seeing her again is frothing up inside me, despite the stark reality that I'm going to be driving her to the police station to turn herself in to face some serious charges. Even after all the pain and hurt she's caused, I find myself wanting to protect her from her inevitable fate, tell her I forgive her, blame my mother for brainwashing her—anything but charge her for her crimes.

I could never have predicted it coming to this. Jess and I had a special connection that I've never experienced with either of my wives. That's why what she's done to me has been so devastating—so hard to fathom. But, like Lexi said, you never really know what someone's capable of until they're pushed to their limits. I certainly didn't know the depths of my own mother's depravity. Or maybe I've been ignoring the truth all these years, dismissing her behavior as petty and harmless until it suddenly became shocking and dangerous. It's hard to admit your own mother is a monster when she's the only parent you've ever known.

"Last chance to change your plans," Will calls to me as he's leaving the office shortly after five-thirty.

"Rain check," I call after him, scrambling to my feet.

I climb into my car and start the engine, my heart

pounding with raw ferocity, a strange mingling of fear and anticipation. As I drive to the park, I fantasize about all the ways I could change this evening's outcome—like taking Jess in my arms and telling her I'm dropping the charges or running away with her and starting over someplace new. Of course that's never going to happen. I love Lexi and Mila too much to hurt them. Whatever mitigating circumstances compelled Jess to do what she did, her behavior is still inexcusable—criminal. She knows that, and she's ready to face the consequences of her actions. My only role is to help make it a reality.

I reach the park ten minutes early and wait in my car with the engine running. I don't want to be the first one to arrive. It makes me look like the desperate wretch I am—chomping at the bit to see her. Jess is the one who should be waiting on me to show up, contrite and eager to make things right. I can't allow myself to view her as anything other than a criminal from now on. I have to keep reminding myself I'm only here to make sure she follows through on her decision to do the right thing.

At exactly 6:00 P.M., I lock my car and walk the short distance to our special spot near the duck pond. A flicker of irritation goes through me when I see our bench is empty. Jess has a nerve making me wait after everything she's done. I scan the surrounding area for any sign of her, but I can't spot her among the dog-walkers or stroller brigade dotting the grassy banks. I walk purposefully past our bench, reluctant to sit there waiting on her, like a salivating puppy. My eye lands on a black trash bag lying in the grass behind the bench, the neck tied in a knot—probably some homeless person's belongings. I walk halfway around the duckpond before turning and heading back in the opposite direction.

It's quarter after six now. I have a sinking feeling Jess has backed out—if she was ever in.

Slumping down on the bench, I drop my head in my hands. All the warm and fuzzy feelings I had for Jess over the course of the afternoon have dissipated. I really believed she was remorseful for what she'd done, but if she can't even be bothered to show up on time, she must be having second thoughts. Unless she decided to drive herself to the station. Or maybe Price has arrested her already. I glance at my phone but there are no messages from either him or Lexi, so I scratch that possibility.

I kick aimlessly at a few pebbles at my feet, trying to ignore the wary glances several of the mothers are beginning to shoot my way. Eventually, I get up and pace around the bench, bending down to take a closer look at the trash bag lying in the grass.

My jaw drops when I see what's written on the note taped to it.

29

LEXI

I clock out of work at 8:00 P.M. and walk out to the parking lot with Stella, my coworker. Despite the hour-long break I had for dinner, my feet are aching after a double shift, but at least I can sleep in tomorrow. I also made several big sales which will land me a nice commission. I'm in good spirits, laughing and joking, when Stella comes to an abrupt halt and holds out an arm in front of me.

"What are you doing?" I laugh, trying to push her aside.

"Your car," she says in a leaden whisper. "It's ..."

She doesn't need to say another word. I've already spotted it in the mottled shadows at the far end of the employee parking section, illuminated by an overhead security light. It looks like it's bleeding from every orifice, red paint pooling onto the asphalt beneath. I walk toward it with an air of trepidation, clapping a hand to my mouth when I read the ghoulish chalk message on the windscreen: *next time it's a knife to your heart.*

I lean against Stella and heave a shaky breath.

"Lexi," she says hesitantly. "You don't think ... Jess did this, do you?"

My coworkers know what's been going on—at least, they know some version of the truth. I haven't told them that Cash's mother might be involved, too. I didn't want to come across as the stereotypical bitter daughter-in-law. Better they hear that directly from Cash.

Stella's acrylic grip digs into my arm. "You need to call the police," she mutters, casting a furtive glance around the parking lot.

I nod numbly, and fish out my phone. I manage to get ahold of Price who promises to be there within thirty minutes. I try Cash's number next, but he doesn't pick up. Fighting a mounting sense of irritation, I leave him a couple of messages, then send him a text. "I don't understand why he's not picking up," I say. "He finished work hours ago. He must have fallen asleep on the couch."

"I can give you a ride home," Stella offers.

"Don't you have to get back to your kids?"

"They're fine," she assures me. "My husband's with them."

TWENTY MINUTES LATER, Price and another officer arrive on the scene. Cash still hasn't called me back, despite me bombarding him with several more messages and texts.

"Are there any functioning cameras in this parking lot?" Price asks, after surveying the damage.

"A couple." I point to the eaves of the store.

He gives an approving nod. "Can we review the footage while we're waiting for the tow truck?"

I make a quick call to my boss to explain what's

happened and secure his permission to take the police into the building.

Back inside the store, I pull up the parking lot camera footage on one of the office computers. We watch in silence as a hooded figure in dark clothing wearing a white plastic cat mask approaches my car at 7:21 P.M. They write on the window, then throw the contents of a can of red paint all over the car, before tossing the empty can into the bushes and darting off into the night.

"Can you identify them—is it a colleague, perhaps?" Officer Price asks.

I shake my head. "No idea."

"I'm guessing it's a woman," Stella says dubiously. "It looks too small to be a man."

I finish making a copy of the footage for Price just as the tow truck rumbles into the parking lot.

"I dread to think how much this is going to cost me," I say. "On top of everything else I've had to fork out to replace the stuff we lost in the bogus garage sale."

"Your auto insurance will cover it," Price replies. "I'll add this incident to your file. Have you had any more interaction with your husband's ex-girlfriend since we last spoke?"

"Nothing since she texted her sister to let her know she was going away for a few weeks."

Price gives a curt nod. "We have a warrant out for her arrest. The minute she uses her credit card or accesses her bank account, we'll nab her."

AFTER I SIGN THE PAPERWORK, and the tow truck takes off with my sorry-looking car, Stella bundles me into her minivan.

"I hope they catch Jess soon," she says. "She deserves

whatever's she's got coming to her after everything she's put you through."

I lean my head up against the car window. "You don't know the half of it."

Stella glances at me quizzically. "I know about the vandalism, and the harassing messages, and the fire at your mother-in-law's—now this. What else is there?"

I grimace. I'm tired of pretending. "For starters, I think the fire was staged. I didn't want to say anything, but Cash and I suspect Eleanor's been in on everything from the beginning."

Stella gawps at me. "Are you kidding me?"

"I wish I were. I know I probably sound like a disgruntled daughter-in-law trying to throw Eleanor under the bus, but we have proof that she sent us at least one harassing card." I pick distractedly at the ragged skin on my thumb. "The truth is, I'm afraid for my life. I think Eleanor schemed with Jess to have someone attack me in the park."

Stella stares at me with a horrified expression. "Does Cash know about your suspicions?"

"He does now. At first, he dismissed it as his mother just being her usual jealous self of the new woman in his life, but it's gone too far for him to ignore. He's seen firsthand the kinds of things his mother does to me."

"If you really think she and Jess were behind the knife attack, aren't you afraid they might try to hurt you again?" Stella asks.

I give a grim nod. "That's why I'm not coming in to work tomorrow. Jess sent a fake obituary with my name on it. The date of my death was tomorrow."

Stella gasps, and swerves, almost hitting a car in the process. "Sorry! You're freaking me out! Do you even want to go home right now? Maybe you shouldn't stay in your house tonight."

"I'll be fine. Cash will be there."

Stella frowns for a long moment, as though choosing her words carefully. "Are you sure he's on your side?"

30

LEXI

The house is in darkness when Stella and I pull up outside. Wade is sitting on his mother's front porch, clutching a can of beer. His gaze swivels unsteadily in our direction.

"I'm not going to leave you here by yourself, if Cash isn't home yet, " Stella hisses at me. "Not with the drunk next-door leering at you like that."

"Let me check if he's on his way." I pull out my phone, but Cash still hasn't responded to any of my messages. "I don't understand why he's not texting me back. I was mad at him earlier, but now I'm getting worried. What if something's happened to him?"

"Could he be working late? How about trying his office number?" Stella suggests.

"No one's going to answer the phone at this time of night. I guess I could try one of his coworkers." I scroll through my contacts and tap on Will's number.

"Yo!" he answers on the third ring. Judging by the racket almost drowning out his voice, he's in a bar somewhere. "Will, it's Lexi. Is Cash with you?"

"No, the wussy said he had something going on." Will laughs and says something else, but it's lost in the cacophony of sound in the background.

"Did he say what?" I yell into the phone.

"Nope. Just that he had plans."

I hang up and turn to Stella with a helpless shrug. "Cash told his coworkers he had something going on, but he didn't say what. Maybe he left in a hurry and forgot his phone at the office. Don't worry, I'll be fine here waiting for him. The house is secure. We have cameras all around the perimeter and ... Cash bought a gun."

Stella's eyes grow wide. "If he thinks you need a gun, this is serious." She reaches for her purse and opens the car door. "If you insist on staying here, I'll wait with you until Cash gets back. I don't care what you say, I'm not leaving you here alone."

I shrug, grab my bag and follow her.

"Ladies night?" Wade calls over to us with an uncoordinated wave.

"Ignore him," I mutter to Stella, as I hurry over to the front door. In my haste, I almost trip over a black trash bag lying on the mat.

"What's that?" Stella asks.

"No idea." I unlock the door and kick the bag aside. "Maybe Cash was taking the trash out and forgot about it."

Stella bends over to inspect it. "It doesn't look like trash to me. There's a note taped to it." She shines her iPhone flashlight on the bag, and sucks in a hard breath. "Lexi, you might want to take a look at this."

I crouch down next to her and read the note aloud. "3042 Hornets Nest Road. Come alone or he ... he dies. Call the police and he dies." I sway backward and Stella grabs me just in time to stop me from falling. She helps me up and escorts me inside, then reaches for the trash bag and pulls it in after us.

"Cash!" is all I manage to whisper, my panicked gaze locked on her.

She ushers me into the kitchen and pushes me gently into a chair. "Don't move! I'm going to call the police right now."

"No! I grab her by the arm and hold on tight. "Please, don't, Stella! I can't risk anything happening to him. This is just Jess playing her sick games again. She wants to make him choose between us. I can handle it. I'll figure something out."

"How? She's stark, raving mad!"

I press my lips tightly together. "I'll take the gun."

Stella closes her eyes and tents her hands over her face. "I can't believe I'm hearing this. Do you even know how to use a gun?"

"Cash showed me."

"*Showed* you! That means nothing. Unless you've practiced using it, I can guarantee you'll never pull it off in the heat of the moment. It's not as easy as you think to shoot someone."

"How do you know?"

She sighs and begins pacing across the floor. "My dad's a marine. He did two tours in Iraq."

I peer at her curiously. "Do *you* know how to use a gun?"

Before she can reply, my phone begins to ring. "It's an unknown number," I whisper, looking to Stella for input. "What should I do?"

"Answer it. If it's her, demand to speak to Cash."

I take a deep breath and hit the speaker. "Hello?"

"Lexi! Are you okay?" Cash blurts out, his tone a mixture of exhilaration and concern.

"Where are you?" I cry. "I've been trying to get ahold of you for hours. I thought for sure Jess had you. Someone left a trash bag on our porch with an address and—"

"Did you open it?" Cash demands.

"Not yet. I—"

"Don't!"

"Why? What's in it?"

"It's just another twisted game she's playing. She texted me earlier claiming she wanted to turn herself in. She told me to meet her at our ... at a bench in the park. When I got there, I found a trash bag with a sweater and a pair of your jeans covered in red paint. At first glance, it looked like blood. I thought for sure she'd followed through on her threat and killed you. In my panic, I dropped my phone on the asphalt and smashed it. I'm calling you from a gas station." He pauses and heaves a breath. "I drove to the address on the bag, but it was just an abandoned building—no trace of Jess."

"Let me guess. 3042 Hornets Nest Road?" I ask.

"Yeah, that's the one," Cash confirms. "Listen to me. She knows you're alone now. You're in danger. I want you to go upstairs and get the gun out of the safe. You locked all the doors, right?"

"I ... I'll do it now. Stella's here—she can help. She gave me a ride home."

Without a word, Stella hurries over to the back door and checks the lock.

"Is everything okay?" Cash asks. "Did you have a flat or something?"

"Someone threw red paint all over my car in the employee parking lot. It's at a body shop right now. Price came out and wrote up a vandalism report."

Cash mutters something unintelligible on the other end

of the line. "There's no way Jess is acting alone. She can't be pulling all this off by herself. I'm on my way home right now. I'll be there as soon as I can. Don't open the door to anyone. When I hang up, I want you to go straight upstairs and get the gun. You remember how to turn the safety off, right?"

"Yes. Drive safe and don't worry about me. Stella knows how to use a gun."

There's a long pause and then Cash says, "Take me off speaker for a minute."

I do as he says and press the phone to my ear. "Okay. What is it?"

"You can't trust anyone," Cash whispers. "Don't let Stella get her hands on that gun."

31

CASH

Despite Lexi's admonition to drive safely, I floor the gas and speed the whole way home, berating myself the entire time for ever giving credence to the notion that Jess might actually be remorseful for what she's done. I can't believe I've been so stupid and allowed myself to be played like a fool. I knew it seemed too easy an end to this nightmare. My immediate concern is that Jess might have recruited Lexi's coworker to offer her a ride home as part of the plan. Jess could be hiding in the house for all I know. Stella almost never works late. It seems too much of a coincidence that tonight, of all nights, she signed up for a double shift alongside Lexi.

Maybe I'm being paranoid, but Jess is brilliant—and my mother is relentless. Between the two of them, they're an unstoppable evil. They've already duped Anya into helping their cause. I'm expecting a letter from her lawyer any day bemoaning her dire situation now that Anton's kicked her to the curb. But money's the least of my worries when Lexi's life is at stake. I wish I could call and check up on her while I drive. I feel lost without my phone, but maybe it's a blessing in disguise it broke before Price got his warrant. The messages between Jess and me could be misconstrued as long as she's technically still missing.

When I finally turn onto my street, an unfamiliar car—Stella's I assume—is parked in the driveway blocking the garage door, so I pull up alongside the curb instead. From his lean-to porch, Wade watches me with a glassy-eyed look. He's obviously spent the evening successfully dulling his senses. Still, there's a chance he might have seen someone dropping off the trash bag at my front door. As soon as I've checked on Lexi, I'll head over there and have a word with him. He raises a beer at me by way of greeting, and I respond with a curt nod before disappearing inside the house. Lexi comes running out of the kitchen and throws her arms around me. "Oh, babe! I wasn't sure I'd ever see you again," she says, choking back a sob.

I press her tightly to me. "Me too. I'm glad you're safe."

Lexi sniffles into my chest. "They wrote on my car window: *next time it's a knife to your heart.* That wasn't a random attack in the park. They're trying to kill me, Cash. They won't rest until they kill me."

"I won't let that happen. Where's the gun?" I whisper in her ear.

She pulls away, a sheepish look on her face. "I'm sorry. I forgot the code for the safe. My mind's in tatters. I thought it was my birthday, or yours, but I punched it in wrong too many times and it locked me out."

"We scrapped that idea in the end," I remind her. "We went with our anniversary instead." I squeeze her gently and ruffle her hair. "Don't worry about it. You're safe now and that's all that matters. We'll sort it out after Stella leaves."

We walk into the kitchen where Stella is seated at the

table with a half-drunk mug of hot chocolate. She glances up briefly from her phone. "Thank goodness you're okay, Cash. Lexi's been beside herself with worry. I'm almost done here. Just texting the kids." Her fingers fly over the keys for another moment or two, and then she sets down her phone.

I smile awkwardly at her. I can't help feeling somewhat guilty for telling Lexi not to trust her, but it was hard not to be paranoid driving back in the dark from that abandoned building, racing to save my wife from imminent death after finding the fake bloody clothes. The truth is, Stella probably saved Lexi's life. If she hadn't stayed with her until I got home, Jess might have seized the opportunity to finish what she started.

"Thank you for stepping up and helping Lexi out this evening," I say. "And for waiting with her until I got back."

"There was no way I was gonna leave her here by herself." Stella gestures to the window. "Not with your creepy neighbor next door watching our every move."

I trace a hand across my brow. "Was he sitting out front when you got back?"

Lexi nods. "Nursing a can and smoking a joint, as usual."

"He might have seen someone dropping the trash bag by the front door. Did you check the cameras, yet?"

"No," Lexi answers. "It probably won't help anyway. We checked the cameras at work and all we could see was a hooded figure wearing this weird cat mask throwing paint over my car—it was impossible to identify them."

"It looked like a woman to me. I told the police as much," Stella says, getting to her feet. "I need to get back to say goodnight to the kids. Let me know if there's anything else I can do to help."

"Will do," Lexi says, hugging her goodbye. "Thanks again for everything."

I walk Stella out to her car and wave her off before heading next door to talk to Wade.

"Pull up a chair, neighbor," he mumbles, flopping a hand in the direction of a broken, canvas deck chair resting against the railing. It doesn't look like it would hold my weight, so I pass. Stuffing my hands into my pockets, I lean back against the wall of the house. "Balmy night, isn't it?"

Wade snorts. "Are you here for the beer, or what?

"No beer, just information. Did you happen to see anyone drop a black trash bag at our front door this evening?"

"A trash bag, huh," Wade says, sounding stumped. "Nope. No trash stalkers in the neighborhood." He laughs at his brilliant joke, then takes a swig of beer and burps.

I take a step toward him and fold my arms across my chest. "How about you, Wade? Have *you* been stalking the neighborhood?"

He scowls, his eyes darting back-and-forth between me and my house. "Are you accusing me of dropping trash on your porch?"

"It wouldn't be the first time you threw trash onto my property, would it?"

He narrows his bloodshot eyes at me. "You oughta watch your back. I could take you out in a heartbeat. And believe me, I'd be doing someone you know a favor."

He makes as though he's going to get up and slug me, but he's too intoxicated to stand. I take a step backward and lean my weight gingerly against the rickety wooden railing.

Biting back my irritation, I try to steer the conversation back on track. "Forget the trash bag. Did you see anyone at our front door this evening?"

Wade frowns and then breaks into a toothy grin. "Oh, yeah, one of those ... what do you call 'em ... furries?"

"Furries?" I repeat in a tone of contempt. I straighten up, preparing to leave. This is obviously a lost cause. He sounds as though he's hallucinating after inhaling too much weed.

"Yeah," Wade says, nodding emphatically. "Hoodie, white cat mask." He laughs raucously. "You got some weird friends."

Back home, I waste no time filling Lexi in on what Wade observed.

"It sounds like the same person who threw paint on my car!" she says in a hushed tone.

A quick check of our exterior camera footage confirms a hooded, masked figure dropping a trash bag onto our front porch around 6:15 P.M. Whoever it is, they're careful not to look directly at the camera, but I catch a glimpse of a white mask of some kind.

I use Lexi's phone to call Price and update him on everything that's happened, including the ploy to lure me and Lexi to an abandoned building.

"I'll need a copy of the footage from your security camera," he says. "I'll see if Tech can enhance it. Where are you now?"

"At home."

"I'll send a patrol car over to cruise the neighborhood just in case the perpetrator is still hanging around. It would be best if you stay put for the rest of the evening."

I end the call and hug Lexi close for a long moment.

"Maybe now you can appreciate why I wanted to buy the gun." I lock a somber gaze on her. "I hope I don't have to use it, but I won't let Jess get close to you again. It's only a matter of time before the police find her and bring her in."

Lexi's shoulders droop. "Your mother will still be out there."

"Maybe not. If Jess agrees to talk in exchange for a plea deal, there's a good chance they'll arrest my mother too. They won't be able to hurt us anymore."

Lexi looks at me doubtfully. "Are you sure you can stand by and watch them both be prosecuted and sentenced? And what if Anya's involved? Are you really going to be able to handle the mother of your child being sent to prison, if it comes to that?"

Cash looks grim. "I'm not saying it will be easy, but if Anya has participated in a crime, she needs to pay for what she's done. The question is, will you be okay with Mila coming to live with us full-time?"

"Of course! You don't even have to ask." Lexi sucks in a small breath. "I just hope we can give her a little brother or sister soon. I know she wants a sibling."

I kiss her softly on the forehead. "I want it too. You have no idea how much I want a family of our own." Releasing her, I glance at the time. "I'm hungry, how about you?"

"I could eat."

"Pizza sound good?" I ask, already tapping on the Door-Dash App on her phone.

"Perfect. Margarita for me, please," Lexi says.

I place the order while she rummages around for paper plates and napkins.

"I found your old phone in the kitchen drawer," she says, bringing it over to me.

"Thanks. I'll order a new one tomorrow. This will get me by in the meantime."

"How long did they say for the pizza?" she asks.

"Thirty minutes." I peer cautiously out through the curtains. "It's going to be pitch dark outside by then. I'm going to get the gun out of the safe and bring it downstairs."

"What for?" Lexi exclaims. "You don't seriously think they've recruited the pizza delivery guy to do their dirty business for them, do you?"

"Of course not. But there's always a risk of something happening when we open the door. What if Jess steps out of the bushes, holds a knife to the delivery guy's throat, and forces her way inside? She has nothing left to lose at this point. She's desperate. I'm not taking any chances. Price warned us she could be hanging around, waiting for a chance to strike."

Lexi gives a resigned shrug. "Okay, if you insist. Just be careful, please."

"Don't worry. I'll keep the gun out of view on the counter. It's just a precaution."

I dart upstairs to the bedroom and punch in the code on the safe. When it beeps, and the lock clicks open, I pull the door toward me. My heart seizes in my chest.

The gun is gone.

"L exi!" Cash yells as he comes thundering back down the stairs. "Where'd you put the gun?"

I frown. "What do you mean? It's in the safe, isn't it?"

"No, it's not! The safe's empty!"

My mouth drops open. "But ..."

"Lexi, think! Did you take it out when Stella was here?"

"No! I couldn't get the safe open. I told you that. I was too flustered. I kept trying numbers and messing it up, and then it locked me out."

Cash's face has turned a mottled gray. "Did Stella know about the gun?"

"What? No! I mean ... I told her you'd bought a gun, but I didn't take her upstairs, or show it to her or anything. She never went near the safe."

Cash plunges a hand into his hair and begins pacing back and forth across the floor. "Who else could have taken it? Who else has been in the house?"

I press my hands to my head. "Only your mom. She was alone here before I got home from the store."

Cash contemplates the idea, then gives a dismissive shake of his head. "No. It couldn't have been her. I didn't arrive home with the gun until after she'd already left. Are you absolutely certain you didn't take it out of the safe?"

"I'm positive! Don't you think I'd remember?"

He throws his arms up. "I don't know. You said yourself you were in panic mode—you couldn't think straight." He flops down on the chair next to me and scrubs his hands over his face. "I'm going to have to report it stolen." He jerks his head up, a startled look in his eyes. "Jess! That must be why she lured me to that address while you were working late. She needed to make sure the house was empty so she could get her hands on the gun."

"But how could Jess have stolen it? She didn't go inside the house. We watched her walk away on the camera."

"Check the app again," Cash urges. "Maybe she came back after we turned the camera off."

He peers over my shoulder as I replay the footage. We watch with bated breath as the masked figure drops the trash bag on the front step, then turns and disappears into the shadows. A minute goes by, then two, before the eerie cat-masked figure reemerges out of the shadows. Cash lets out a yelp and jabs at the screen. "I told you! I knew it!"

We watch in shocked silence as the figure reaches up and punches a code into the entry keypad, then disappears into the house.

I dig my nails into the cushion I'm holding on my lap. "I can't believe what I just saw! This might not be the first time she's been inside our house. She could have been the one who bleach-bombed my clothes. But how did she know the code?"

"Mom must have given it to her, as well as the garage code," he says, furiously working his jaw side-to-side.

"But we didn't tell anyone the code for the safe." I shake my head in bewilderment. "How did Jess even know we had a gun in the first place?"

Cash throws me a sheepish look. "I told Mom about the gun when I chewed her out for destroying your wedding dress, remember?"

I bite my lip. "And she knows we typically use our anniversary or one of our birthdays for all our passwords. It wasn't hard to figure out."

Cash sets his jaw in a hard line. "We can't stay here tonight. Not without the gun."

"But Price said he'd have an officer patrolling the neighborhood," I remind him. "Jess isn't going to try anything with a police cruiser in the area."

Cash snorts. "Now who's underestimating her?"

The doorbell rings and we freeze, staring at each other like we're playing a game of musical statues.

"It's probably just the pizza delivery," I say, with a slight tremor in my voice.

"It doesn't matter. We're not opening the door now—not for anyone," Cash replies firmly. He walks over to the front door and yells through it. "You can leave the pizza on the doorstep, thanks."

"Gotcha. You all have a good evening!" the delivery guy yells back.

I peek through the blinds and watch him jog back down the driveway to his car and speed off. "Okay," I say. "He's gone now."

I walk over to the door to retrieve the food, but Cash grabs me by the arm and spins me around to face him. "Forget the pizza. It's not worth the risk."

"I really think you're overreacting," I say, shaking myself

free of him. "It will just take two seconds to grab it. I'm starving."

His eyes flash with anger. "Overreacting—are you serious? Jess broke into our house tonight and stole our gun! She's made it clear she wants to get rid of you—both of us—if I don't comply with her demands. She's armed and dangerous. Even Price advised us to stay inside."

I throw up my hands in frustration. "Fine. I'll make sandwiches—let the pizza rot. The neighborhood dogs are in for a treat."

I'm slathering mayonnaise on brown bread in a disgruntled fashion when Helen calls.

"Lexi, dear, are you all right? Wade told me you had an intruder this evening."

"I'm fine, thanks. Fortunately, we weren't home when they came in."

"Well, that's a blessing, I suppose. I'm so sorry this has happened right on the heels of the garage sale fiasco. I hope they didn't do any damage or take anything."

I glance hesitantly over my shoulder to make sure Cash isn't within earshot. "They stole a loaded handgun out of the safe in our bedroom."

Helen lets out a breathy gasp. "How frightening! How did they manage to break open your safe?"

"That's the really scary part—they didn't. They knew the code."

There's a long pause before Helen responds. "Who discovered the gun was missing?"

"Cash. He went upstairs to get it this evening. He wanted to have it near at hand in case the intruder came back."

"I see," Helen says. Her tone has changed—charged with a foreboding air. "Lexi, please be careful. That gun might still be in the house."

34

CASH

The following morning, Jess's sister Naomi calls when I'm getting ready for work. I grimace, debating whether or not to take the call. I'm shattered after spending half the night on edge, listening for the sound of a door creaking open or footsteps coming up the stairs.

"I need to talk to you," she says.

"Better make it quick. I'm about to head out the door," I reply, making no attempt to mask my irritation as I hit the speaker button on my old iPhone. Thanks to her feeding misinformation to the police, I've already endured a grilling from Price about my involvement in Jess's disappearance. I've got a feeling it won't be the last. As far as he's concerned, I have motive—my unhinged ex is making my life miserable. His antenna is up now, and it's always the boyfriend, after all.

"I'm scared something bad has happened to Jess," Naomi begins. "I'm afraid for her."

"And I'm afraid *of* her," I reply, combing gel through my hair. "She's deranged and dangerous."

"Something isn't right," Naomi goes on, ignoring my hostile tone as her words tumble out in breathless succession. "She would never disappear like this without telling me."

"But she did tell you," I remind her. "She texted you, remember?"

"That's just it. I'm not sure it was her."

I stare at my reflection in the bathroom mirror, mesmerized by the dark circles I've acquired of late. They make me look older, and not in a sexy way. Decidedly more haggard. "I'm lost. You told me Jess texted you."

"I know, but here's the thing. I messaged her on Facebook about our cousin's wedding—just to be sure she'd be back in time for the shower. She responded, but it was a weird message. It didn't sound like her at all. She even spelled our cousin's name wrong. So then I messaged her again saying how much I loved the teal blue bridesmaids' dresses, and she replied that she loved them too. The thing is, they're not teal blue!"

I scratch the back of my head, trying to connect the dots, as I poke and prod at the bags beneath my eyes. "So?"

"She's in the wedding, Cash! She's a bridesmaid. She knows the dresses are champagne rose!"

I frown, digesting the information. "So what are you saying?"

Naomi exhales in exasperation. "I'm saying I don't think Jess is the one texting me, which means someone else is using her phone, which indicates she's in trouble."

"Or she's had a psychotic break! Did you ever consider that possibility? Why else would she tell you she was dropping everything, her PhD included, to go off traveling, when there's a warrant out for her arrest? She trashed Lexi's car, broke into our house, and stole my handgun. She wants me back—she told me that straight out—and if I don't give her what she wants, she'll kill me and everyone around me."

"Cash, you know her better than anyone. Does that sound remotely like Jess to you?"

I heave out a ragged breath. "It sounds like a disturbed person, which is what she's become. Some smart people have a proclivity to madness. She hid it well, until now. I think Jess needs some heavy-duty psychiatric help."

My head is pounding by the time I get off the phone with Naomi. None of what she said made any sense, and yet, something about it niggles at me. If it wasn't Jess texting, then who was it? Who was it on the cameras trashing Lexi's car and breaking into our house? I know Mom has done some pretty shocking things of late—even deigning to purchase a box of tacky cards and send a sick message—but I can't picture her in a cat mask, sweatpants, and a hoodie. Then again, I've been seriously miscalculating the lengths she's willing to go to to get what she wants.

Despite my contention that Jess might have experienced a psychotic break, Naomi's call has got me rethinking everything. A knot forms in my throat as a terrible thought occurs to me. What if Mom retaliated against Jess when she said she wanted to turn herself in? If Mom hired someone to stab Lexi, she could just as easily have hired someone to kidnap Jess, or worse. She could even be using Jess's phone to send those messages—making her the scapegoat for everything that's been happening. I lean over the sink, suddenly sick to my stomach. Could my own mother be responsible for Jess's disappearance?

Lexi knocks on the bathroom door. "Cash? Are you almost done in there?"

"Be right out," I answer. My voice sounds strangled and guilt-ridden. I can't tell Lexi about Naomi's suspicions. She

won't want to entertain the idea that Jess might be an innocent party in all of this. She'll accuse me of taking her side
or being more concerned about my ex-girlfriend than my
own wife. The truth is, after hearing what Naomi had to say,
I am worried for Jess. It never sat right with me that she
could flip the script entirely and become a green-eyed
monster overnight, willing to stoop to criminal acts to
destroy me. My mother, on the other hand, has never shied
away from unscrupulous behavior to achieve her purposes.

"Are you feeling okay?" Lexi asks, when I finally open
the bathroom door. She eyes me dubiously. "You look pale. I
hope you're not coming down with something."

I shake my head. "Just stressed, that's all."

"Who was that you were talking to on the phone?"

I button up the sleeve on my shirt, avoiding her scrutinizing gaze. "Naomi. Jess's sister."

Lexi folds her arms in front of her. "Has Jess been in
touch with her?"

I give a tight nod. "Sort of. Naomi messaged her on Facebook to make sure she'd be back in time for their cousin's
wedding. She says Jess's responses raised a big, red flag.
She's in the wedding but she didn't know the color of the
bridesmaids' dresses, and she misspelled her cousin's name.
Naomi's got it into her head that someone else is using Jess's
phone to send those messages. Personally, I think everything points to Jess having some kind of mental breakdown.
It does make you wonder though."

Lexi tucks a strand of hair carefully behind her ear, her
brow furrowing. "I suppose if it were my sister, I would want
to believe the best of her, too. But we both know that's naive.
We saw her on our camera going into our house."

"We saw *someone* on our camera," I correct her.

"Okay, if it wasn't Jess, who was it?"

I twist my lips into a grimace, the gears in my brain whirring. "Mom has a vendetta against you, too."

"That's ridiculous! Dressing like a homeless person's a step too far for Eleanor!"

"I'm not saying it was her. But she could have recruited someone to do her bidding—someone who owes her, and who sees you as an obstacle to getting more money out of me."

Lexi gasps, as it suddenly dawns on her. "Anya!" she says in a breathless whisper. "But she hates Eleanor."

I give a grim nod, recalling Anya's ill-omened words. "True, but drastic times call for drastic measures."

35

CASH

Once I reach the office, I text Anya and tell her we need to meet to talk about Mila. It's merely a ploy to get her on her own and confront her about my suspicions, without my mother hovering in the background. She doesn't respond right away, so I do my best to concentrate on the design plan I'm currently working on. Things have been piling up on my desk, and I've let a few things slide through the cracks which have come to the attention of my boss. I need to remedy that before a neglected client starts kicking up a fuss. I've already taken too much time off work lately. I can't afford to lose my job on top of everything else.

When I break for lunch, Will and I head out to a nearby cafe we frequent. I've just taken a bite of my roast beef and provolone sandwich when my phone begins to buzz. I can't handle a tirade from Anya right now. I'll deal with her back in the privacy of my office. I keep chewing, ignoring my phone until it falls silent. A moment later, it starts up again.

"Aren't you going to get that?" Will asks.

"It can wait," I say. "This sandwich has my attention right now—it's killer."

"Might be the boss. You're skating on thin ice, as it is," Will replies, through a mouthful of turkey. "Whoever's calling, they're pretty insistent."

Reluctantly, I pull out my phone and check the screen.

Did you really think you could shoot me?

I set down my sandwich, suddenly sick to my stomach.

Will raises his brows and stops chewing. "Everything okay?"

I rub a hand over my jaw. "It's my psycho ex. She's been threatening me and my wife. There's a warrant out for her arrest."

Will whistles softly. "Yikes! I knew she was harassing you guys, but I had no idea it had gone that far. You've got some crazy stuff going on, bro." He gestures with his chin to my phone. "What's she saying now?"

I set the phone on the table between us and spin it around to face him. "This is pretty typical—more of her usual deranged nonsense. At least I think it's her. The messages always come from a burner phone. Her sister's trying to convince me that someone else is pretending to be her and sending the texts. She thinks she's in trouble."

Will reads the message in silence, then wipes his fingers on a napkin, his face pinched in concentration. "Text her back. Tell her to prove it's really her."

"How?"

"I dunno. Have her call you."

"She won't do that. I've already asked. She doesn't want me trying to trace the call."

"Tell her to send you a picture of something only she would have. Her driver's license, maybe?"

I push my half-eaten sandwich to one side. "It wouldn't

prove anything. If someone's kidnapped her, it stands to reason they have her purse and driver's license too."

Will shrugs. "There must be something she can do to prove it's her."

"Yeah, maybe," I say, glancing at my watch. "We should get back to the office. I need to get the amendments on my bridge design plan finished up. I have a meeting with the client tomorrow."

Halfway through the afternoon, Price calls me. "Your mother's court case is set for this Friday at 11:00 A.M. Can you be there?"

I swallow the bile rising up my throat. It brings me no pleasure to anticipate testifying against my own mother, despite knowing it's the right thing to do. "I should be able to swing it. What do you think will happen to her?"

"With no prior record, there's a chance she could walk away with an order to pay restitution and complete a few hours of community service."

"It would do her good to spend a few days in jail reflecting on what she's done," I say grimly.

Price is silent for a moment. "Do you still suspect she was involved in the knife attack on your wife?"

"Sadly, yes. She may even have masterminded it. But that's just speculation on my part. I have no way of proving it. Any leads on finding Jess?"

"No. We're searching for her car but, so far, the plates haven't shown up anywhere."

I let out a snort of reluctant admiration. "She's too clever to get caught like that. She's either changed them out by now, or she's using a different car."

After asking Price to keep me apprised of any developments, I end the call. Not that I believe he will follow through on my request. I'm pretty sure I'm still a suspect in

Jess's disappearance. But with nothing to indicate foul play, he has nothing to hold me on.

I stare at the phone in my hand, rereading the most recent message from the burner phone. It's an admission that whoever sent it stole my gun. They want me to know they've taken away my power and have the upper hand. I can't help thinking about what Will said at lunch. I need proof Jess has been sending the messages. If she's in trouble —if my mother has done something to her—I have to help her. She has no one else.

Before I can talk myself out of it, I message back, asking for a photo to prove it's really her; *a selfie, your driver's license, a gift I gave you, the more items the better.*

It's almost an hour later before I receive a response.

As I open up the attached photos, my skin begins to crawl.

The first one is a close-up of the serial number on the side of a handgun—*my handgun,* along with Jess's driver's license, a credit card, and a knife.

The second photo is Jess standing on a beach grinning broadly at the camera.

In the far corner of the third photo, a blond-haired woman lies bound and gagged. The text across the photo reads: *In loving memory of the second Mrs. Reisinger.*

36

LEXI

Cash has been acting very strangely, fluctuating between being clingy and controlling one minute, and distant and unresponsive the next. He called me from work in a blind panic a couple of days ago asking if I was okay and warning me to keep the doors locked until he got home. I know testifying at his mother's trial was stressful for him, but he was determined to see it through. I couldn't tell if he was relieved or disappointed when the judge ended up ordering Eleanor to do thirty hours of community service in lieu of jail time for the trespassing charge. The vandalism charge was thrown out entirely as we had no conclusive proof it was her who destroyed my wedding dress. She's back living in her own house now, along with Anya and Mila. It's far from an ideal situation, but Cash is trying to make the best of it for his daughter's sake.

"Have you confronted Anya, yet, about taking the gun?" I ask Cash that evening over dinner. I've been bugging him to do it, but he's dragging his feet. She's suing him for more child support, and he's afraid she'll hit him with a defamation suit, if he brings up the stolen gun, and accuses her of breaking and entering. We told Price about our suspicions regarding Anya's involvement, but to say he was skeptical is an understatement. I get the feeling we're beginning to irritate him with our toxic triangle theories. It's a two-way street. His mindless incompetence gets under my skin.

"It's not that easy," Cash says, in a defeated tone. "She's refusing to meet with me. She told me her lawyer would be in touch and I could talk to him. All she wants right now is more money. The last thing I want to do is antagonize her any further. She might decide to sue for full custody just to spite me. I can't put Mila through that kind of legal wrangling. She's facing enough upheaval as it is." He swallows a mouthful of mashed potatoes, not quite meeting my eyes.

I set down my fork and stare across the table at him until the silence becomes too much to bear and he looks up at me. "That's not the real reason you haven't confronted Anya, is it? What is it you're not telling me?"

He rubs his jaw, clearly uncomfortable.

I fold my arms in front of me on the table. "This has something to do with Jess, doesn't it? I can tell by the look on your face."

He pulls out his phone with a sigh and passes it to me. "I got another message from her a couple of days ago. I don't know who the woman tied up with her back to the camera is —it could even be Anya posing with a blond wig. I don't trust her—she betrayed me before. I'm pretty sure they wanted me to think they had you bound and gagged. If nothing else, they were sending a clear message of what they'd like to do to you. That's why I've been a bit overprotective lately, calling and checking on you at work and stuff."

I stare at the photos for a long moment, then hand him back the phone. "Why did she send you these?"

"I asked her for proof she was behind the messages."

"And now you have it," I say grimly. "You need to show these photos to Price."

"But what if Naomi's right and it's not her?" he asks, his eyes glistening. "That means whoever's pretending to be her has my gun and the knife too. Jess could be in real danger."

"She doesn't look like she's in danger. She's smiling in that one picture—like the cat who got the cream."

Cash rubs his knuckles in an agitated fashion. "That's an old picture from a vacation we took to Maui. It doesn't mean she's safe."

My stomach begins to churn in an all too familiar way. "You're still trying to protect her, aren't you? It's always about Jess. It's always been about her, hasn't it?"

Cash raises his hands defensively. "Lexi, please don't be like this."

"Like what? Hurt that my husband cares more about his crazed ex-girlfriend than his wife?"

"That's not true and you know it!"

I shake my head. "We both know how you really feel about Jess. Eleanor's right. You would do anything for her—lie, cheat, or steal."

Cash gets to his feet, his chair screeching over the floor. "I don't have to sit here and listen to this anymore. I'm going to pick up Mila. If you don't like how I'm handling things, you can stay here and fend for yourself."

Before I can stop him, he storms out of the house, letting the door slam behind him.

37

LEXI

My eyes burn as I fight to hold back tears. I hate that I'm not enough for Cash. He still wants her. After everything that's gone down, he still wants Jess. In a bizarre kind of way, I think he wants her more now than ever. I've given him everything, yet he barely acknowledges the sacrifices I've made. She could throw him a scrap and he'd come running back, begging for more like a dumb, abused dog that doesn't know any better. He can't see her for what she's become. It's all wrong, and I don't know how to fix it.

I get to my feet and begin loading the dishwasher to distract myself from thinking about Jess any longer. At least Cash appears to have finally broken the toxic bond with his mother. To my knowledge, they haven't spoken to each other since she was charged. I'm not sure that's a good thing. It could be giving her more fodder to stew on, a greater incentive to dream up a plan for revenge. No doubt, she blames me for destroying her relationship with her son. It won't take much on her part to persuade Anya to help her now that she's living on her nickel. Unlike me, Anya can be bought.

The only person I feel who's really one-hundred percent on my side is Helen. She has always looked out for my best interests, which is sweet of her. But it's also frustrating that she seems more mistrustful of Cash than of his exes. She's made a couple of comments that alarmed me, and I'm afraid she might have passed on her suspicions to Price. I don't like the direction his conversations are taking lately either—insinuating Cash had something to do with Jess's disappearance. He even threatened to get a warrant for Cash's phone, although, I don't know if he ever followed through on it. Maybe now's a good time for me to have a heart-to-heart with Helen while Cash is picking up Mila. Helen means well, but she's barking up the wrong tree, suspecting Cash of something nefarious.

I ring the doorbell several times, but no one answers. I know Helen's home because she's always home in the evenings—she's usually in bed by eight and it's six-thirty now. I walk around through the side gate to the back of the house and peer through the kitchen window, but there's no sign of her anywhere. She can't have gone to bed already. I throw a quick glance over my shoulder at the detached garage behind the house. I can't see any light peeking through the crack in the filthy curtains that hang askew in the windows. I'm reluctant to knock on Wade's door—something I've avoided doing until now—but I have no choice. I need to check on Helen, like a good neighbor would.

I take a breath to steady my nerves, my footsteps crunching over the gravel as I approach the garage. A shiver crosses my shoulders. Cash would kill me if he knew what I was doing. Kill is a poor choice of words, all things considered, but he would be furious to discover I'd taken such a risk. Come to think of it, he's been angry a lot lately. I sense the pressure's getting to him, which is another reason we need to move away from here and make a fresh start someplace new.

I stand in front of Wade's door, my heartbeat growing more insistent, before lifting a fist and rapping loudly. There's no turning back now. I shift impatiently from one foot to the other. It doesn't come as much of a surprise when no one answers. When Wade's not lounging on Helen's porch, he's either drinking in some pub, or passed out on his couch. I'm about to hammer on the door again when it suddenly swings open. A bleary-eyed Wade peers out at me, blinking himself awake. "Huh?" He rubs his scruffy jaw and scowls at me. "What are *you* doing here?"

"Your mother's not answering her door. Do you know if she's gone to bed?"

Wade yawns, saliva dripping from his rotten teeth like some kind of bacteria-ridden reptile. "How would I know?"

"The lights are all out in her house. Maybe you should check on her."

He lifts his shirt and scratches his belly, staring at me in a way that makes me increasingly uncomfortable. I take a small step away from the door. I'm pretty sure I could outrun him if it came down to it, but I want to be prepared.

"Yeah, whatever," he says, at length, tottering out through the doorway.

I follow him up to the main house and through the back door into the kitchen. A stale odor permeates the space, as though the room hasn't been aired out in months.

"Ma! You awake?" Wade yells, tromping across the kitchen floor. He leads me into the downstairs bedroom, before coming to an abrupt halt. I peer tentatively around him, then let out a horrified shriek when I spot Helen lying crumpled on the floor alongside her bed.

"She's fallen! Call 911!" I yell, as I dart by Wade and drop to my knees at his mother's side. It doesn't look good. One half of her face is completely black and blue. I check for a pulse. It's weak but she's alive and conscious. Her eyes flicker in recognition when I lean over her.

Finally, Wade seems to grasp the seriousness of the situation, and fumbles for the phone next to the bed. I do my best to make Helen comfortable while Wade struggles to relay the necessary information to the emergency responders.

Within minutes, the paramedics are onsite. I step aside to allow them to attend to Helen. Wade stands in the doorway, alternately scratching his head and his belly. He's acting perplexed, but his eyes are shifty, as though assessing the situation and what this will mean for him.

As the paramedics wheel Helen out to the waiting ambulance, she lifts a frail arm in my direction. I lean down and whisper to her, "You're okay, Helen. Everything's going to be all right now."

She digs her bony fingers into my arm and rasps, "Someone ... pushed ... me."

38

CASH

I try doing some deep breathing exercises on my way to pick up Mila, but it doesn't work. By the time I turn onto my mother's street, my tension has ratcheted up another level. I still can't believe she allowed Anya to move in, after everything she's said about her in the past. They got off on the wrong foot from the very beginning—both being equally selfish and opinionated. At least Lexi tried to get along with Mom, even though she got shot down at every opportunity. Jess fared a little better, but I think Mom was secretly jealous of her. She knew how much Jess meant to me, and she couldn't stand not being the most important woman in my life.

Maybe I'm still being naïve, but I can't help thinking Jess is in trouble. The fact that the police haven't been able to find any trace of her or her car since they issued a warrant for her arrest is unsettling. Naomi told me she hasn't used any of her credit cards or withdrawn any money from her bank account either—all signs that something is seriously amiss. If she really has gone on the run, why would she still be hanging out in the area, breaking and entering, stealing my handgun, messaging me and Naomi?

I pull up outside my mother's house and steel myself before climbing out to face the fray. The minute the front door opens, Mila hurtles through it and throws herself into my arms.

"Daddy!" She wraps her chubby hands tightly around my neck, and I melt into her sweet embrace. I've missed my baby girl so much these past couple of months. Between the trip to Europe, the stalking, the knife attack, the miscarriage, and the house fire, we've barely been able to spend any time together. And now, Anya's threatening to file for full custody, citing the dangerous situation our daughter is exposed to at my house as grounds. I've already received paperwork from her lawyer that I need to respond to. It all boils down to money, of course. The more time Mila spends with Anya, the more I'm obligated to pay her. I don't give a hoot about the increased child support, but I'll use every last penny I have to fight a custody suit. And if I find out that Anya was involved in any of the criminal harassment Lexi and I have endured, I'll take her to court and have her declared an unfit mother. Lexi's already assured me she would be thrilled if Mila came to live with us full-time. And once all of this is behind us, we can try for another child—a sibling for Mila—to complete our family.

"Are you having fun at Nana's?" I ask, as I buckle Mila into her car seat.

"Yep. But I miss my pink room."

"You have a pink room at my house," I remind her.

She sighs, letting her chin rest on her chest. "But not my big pink room."

I recoil inwardly, partly at the reminder that I can never measure up to Anton's exclusive accommodations, complete with infinity pool, and bowling alley in the basement. And partly at the idea that Mila might be absorbing some of her mother's lust for money.

"How about we play a game of hide and go seek when we get home?" I suggest—opting for distraction rather than a lecture about the value of relationships over material things.

"Yay!" Mila shrieks, kicking the back of my seat in her excitement.

I grin at her in the rearview mirror, my heart swelling. If only it were as easy to keep all the women in my life happy.

When we arrive home, there's no sign of Lexi anywhere. I shoot her a quick text while Mila runs to her room to hide. A moment later, my phone pings with a response.

At the hospital with Helen. I'll keep you posted.

I'm about to text back when I hear Mila yelling for me. I grimace and set down my phone. Whatever the news about Helen is, it can wait for a minute. Lexi's with her so she's in good hands. I need to make my daughter my priority now that I finally have the opportunity to be alone with her.

"Coming!" I call back.

We spend the next few minutes alternately hiding and hunting for each other before Mila decide she needs a snack.

"Didn't you just eat dinner at Nana's?" I ask.

She shrugs. "I didn't like it."

"Okay, what would you like for a snack?"

"Peanut butter crackers and apple juice."

"Aren't you forgetting something?"

"*Pl-ease!*"

"Okay, take your iPad into the family room and I'll bring your snack in when it's ready."

She scampers off out of the room, while I hunt for the jar of peanut butter at the back of the pantry.

As I reach for it, a loud crack reverberates through the house and the kitchen window shatters.

39

CASH

"Mila!" I scream, as the jar of peanut butter falls from my grip. I dash into the family room to gather my terrified daughter into my arms before racing upstairs for cover. Safely inside the bathroom, I lock the door, then dial 911.

"Someone just shot at our house! They shattered the kitchen window. I'm here with my six-year-old daughter," I rattle off to the emergency dispatcher. "You need to get someone out here right now." I recite my address as I rock Mila back-and-forth in my lap.

"I want Mommy!" she wails.

"Shhh! I know, baby," I soothe, pressing her to my chest. "Everything's going to be all right."

The dispatcher stays on the line with me until the comforting sound of sirens fills the air.

Within minutes the house is abuzz with police and emergency responders, floodlights lighting up the backyard. My mind is a blur as I repeat my story to the officer taking my statement. The questions come thick and fast. *Do you know anyone who might want to harm you? Have you received any threats? Do you have any enemies? Have you noticed any strangers hanging around lately?* I do my best to give the officer a brief rundown of the situation, but my mind's too much of a jumble to string a coherent sentence together, so I end up asking him to call Price.

At some point in the midst of the commotion, Anya appears in my kitchen, eyes glinting as she snatches Mila from my arms. "It's pretty clear now who the unfit parent is. You'll be hearing from my lawyer!" she hisses.

Mila buries her face in her mother's neck, whimpering as Anya marches out to her car with her. I watch from the doorway as they drive off. I have a sinking feeling it might be the last time I'll be allowed to have my daughter at my house, unsupervised.

My phone chirps with an incoming message and I glance at it hesitantly, expecting it to be Anya unloading on me some more.

How do you like me now? J

I clutch my phone to my stomach as though I've taken a punch to the gut and stagger backward. A paramedic spots me and grabs me by the elbow. "Sir, are you all right?"

"I ... yes ... I just need to sit down, thanks."

He helps me to a chair, checks my pulse, and observes me for a minute before taking off again. I stare at the message on my phone in shock and disbelief. Is this Jess's way of admitting she shot at me? Did she know my daughter was with me? She must have known it was a possibility, but she shot into my house anyway. As the realization hits, I feel nothing but intense loathing for her.

I take a few deep breaths to clear my head and then call Lexi.

"Hey!" she answers. "Did you get my text? Helen's in surgery. The doctor thinks she took a fall. She smashed her head pretty badly." She hesitates. "The weird thing is Helen thinks someone pushed her. She's probably just confused due to the concussion."

"Oh."

"Cash? Are you ... okay?"

"I ... no. Someone shot at the house this evening, the kitchen window's shattered. I was making Mila a snack. She ... she could have been killed." My voice breaks and I drop my head into my hands.

"What? Are you serious? Is Mila okay?"

I try to say something, but my throat feels like it's closing over, and all that comes out is a garbled sound.

"Cash, talk to me! Please!" Lexi begs, her voice escalating in pitch with every syllable.

"She's ... fine. We're both fine. Anya came and picked her up already. The police are here right now."

"We can't stay there tonight," Lexi says in a decisive tone. "Not with a shooter on the loose."

"Where else are we supposed to go at this time of night? Tom has family in town. We can't go to my mother's. Anya's not going to let me come anywhere near Mila ever again if she can help it." Despite my best efforts to keep a grip on my emotions, I start sobbing.

"We can get a hotel room," Lexi replies. "I'm coming home right now and we'll figure something out."

"What about Helen?"

"I'll leave my number and ask the hospital to call me once she's out of surgery. Wade took off hours ago. The loser only hung around for a few minutes—he didn't even wait to talk to the doctor."

I frown. "I wonder where he went. He hasn't come home yet."

Lexi lets out a disgusted snort. "Indulging his habit, I bet. He couldn't care less about his mother."

An uneasy feeling goes through me. "What time did he leave the hospital?"

"I don't know. Before Helen went into surgery. A couple of hours ago, at least."

I hang up with Lexi and immediately call Price. "I think you should talk to my neighbor, Wade, about the shooting. He threatened me a few days ago."

"Probably just the drink talking," Price answers curtly. "He was inebriated when I interviewed him."

"I'm not so sure. He made a weird comment about doing someone I know a favor. What if Jess gave him the gun?"

40

LEXI

It's been a slow afternoon so far at work, and I'm left with too much time to dwell on my dark thoughts. Helen fell into a coma after the surgery and hasn't regained consciousness yet. I've been checking my phone incessantly over the past few days in case there are any updates from the hospital, but nothing so far. Wade finally showed up last night, but Cash has warned me to steer clear of him. He's worried Jess might have given him the gun and paid him to shoot out the window. He also suspects Wade might have clocked his own mother during one of his drunken tirades over money. I told him Wade was acting shifty when the paramedics arrived. The police interviewed him again, but he denied any involvement in either incident.

After going back-and-forth on the issue, Cash and I moved back into our house last night. The window has been replaced, but I'm still finding tiny pieces of glass under the cabinets on the kitchen floor—jagged reminders that there's a killer on the loose.

My phone beeps, and a text message from Naomi pops up.

Do you know where Cash is? I'm trying to reach him but he's not answering my texts.

I tap out a response. *He's at a job site with a client this morning. What's up?*

I'm curious what she's bugging him about now, but I don't expect her to divulge anything to me. To my surprise, she texts back right away.

Jess was a no show at the bridal shower. Please tell him I need to talk to him ASAP.

I slip my phone into my pocket and move to the cash register to ring up a customer. Did she really think Jess was going to show up to their cousin's bridal shower, knowing there was a warrant out for her arrest? Naomi seems like such a dolt—I guess Jess got all the brains in the family.

I've no sooner finished bagging up my customer's purchase when Price calls. He clears his throat in his usual off-putting manner before getting to the point. "I need you to come down to the station."

My breath clogs like cotton wool. "What for? I'm at work at the moment."

"Can you take off early? It's important."

My heart begins to race a little faster. "Can you at least tell me what this is about?"

"I'd prefer to discuss it in person."

"Okay. I ... I'll see what I can do," I stutter, before hanging up. My palms are sweating. This must have something to do with Jess. Has he had a breakthrough in the case?

"What's going on?" Stella asks, folding sweaters in deft moves as she talks.

"Price wants to talk to me down at the station."

Stella's eyes grow wide. "Do you think they've made an arrest?"

"I doubt it. He was being evasive. I'm not sure what he wants."

"Go!" Stella says, shooing me away with her hands. "Maybe they've got a lead on Jess's whereabouts. It's dead here this afternoon anyway. I can handle things while you're gone."

"Are you sure?"

"Positive! Fingers crossed, it's good news. You can tell me all about it tomorrow."

Sweat prickles along the back of my neck as I drive to the station. I try texting Cash several times but, unsurprisingly, he doesn't respond—he won't be done with his client until noon. I'm trying to envision what Price could possibly want to tell me that requires a face-to-face meeting. Have they found Jess? No! He would have told me that over the phone. Hopefully, he's not dragging me in to tell me something completely inconsequential. Sometimes, I could put my hands around that dimwit's neck and throttle him. He should have had this case wrapped up by now. I want nothing more than to put our house on the market and move away from here as soon as possible. Instead, I'm stuck here until Cash is cleared of any wrongdoing.

I check my phone one last time before walking into the police station. Naomi has texted me again, asking if I got ahold of Cash. I ignore the message, not wanting her to know that he hasn't texted me back either.

I take a seat in Price's office. He nods curtly before tenting his pudgy fingers on the desk in front of him and blinking solemnly across at me. "Thanks for getting here so promptly."

I shrug. "I hope this won't take long. I had to get someone to cover for me at work."

Ignoring my comment, Price reaches for a file on his desk and flips it open. "We've had a development in the case."

I sit up a little straighter, my skin prickling. "What kind of development?"

"We found Jess's car."

I stare at him in shock for a long moment, before gathering my thoughts. "And Jess ... I mean ... was she in it?"

"No."

I frown. "Did she abandon it somewhere?"

Price coughs into his fist. "We don't believe so. The car was discovered deep in the woods covered with branches. I'm afraid there was evidence of foul play. Traces of blood on the seat."

I cover my mouth with my hands, trying to rally my thoughts. "Was it ... her blood?"

Price gives a laborious nod. "Yes. We also found several hairs we believe belong to her assailant." His eyes drill into mine. "I'm afraid the samples are a match to your husband's."

"Were you aware of any ongoing relationship between your husband and Jessica Spicer," Price asks.

"What? No! I mean they were ... friends, but ... " My voice trails off and I shudder as Price's eyes light up in anticipation.

"I need to warn you we can charge you with obstruction of justice if we find out you're impeding the investigation in any way."

"I'm not!" I cry. "You're mistaken. I mean, they kept in touch. Cash and Jess used to date. Why wouldn't his hair be in her vehicle?"

Price blinks at me in a predatory fashion. "It was mixed with her blood."

I tighten my jaw. "I don't believe it! That can't be true! You've got this all wrong. This is Jess's doing. She's setting him up, don't you see? She's jealous of our relationship, she's trying to punish him for not getting back with her."

Price raises a brow and jots something down on the file

in front of him. "I understand this is coming as a shock to you, but your husband has been on our radar ever since Jessica Spicer disappeared."

"No!" I say, shaking my head adamantly. "You're mistaken. She's doing this. This is a set up to frame Cash. She's been sending him threatening messages, trying to sabotage our relationship in all sorts of sick ways, making our lives miserable. You know what she's put us through. You have all the reports." I pause and gulp in a breath. "Cash thinks his mother has been helping her." I lean across the desk and hold Price's gaze. "She gave Jess the code to our gun safe. She's the only one who could have known it. It's hardly a coincidence that someone shot at Cash and his daughter this past weekend. Jess is out there somewhere, armed and dangerous."

Price lets out a humph. "Ah, yes. I was getting to the shooting. I'm afraid your husband's story doesn't add up. First, he tried to convince me it was Jess who shot at your house. Now he's trying to pin it on your next-door neighbor, Wade. But the reality is, you have no proof that anyone stole your gun. Your husband was the one who discovered it was missing, is that right?"

I shrink back from the accusatory look in his eyes. I was right. Helen must have told him about her suspicions. "Why does it matter?"

Price blinks impassively at me. "Your husband discovered the gun was missing, and then he told you someone shot at the kitchen window—neither of which you witnessed." He narrows his eyes at me. "Doesn't that strike you as odd?"

My lips flap but nothing comes out. I'm beginning to think there are more gears whirring in Price's head than I realized. But he's coming to the wrong conclusions.

"We've confirmed the gun used in the shooting belonged to your husband," he breezes on, without waiting for an answer.

"It was stolen! We reported it stolen!" I yell, infuriated by his dogged pursuit of Cash's guilt.

"We?" Price eyes me skeptically before consulting the file in front of him. "It was your husband who reported it stolen. We've already established that you didn't accompany him upstairs to the safe, so you would have had no way of knowing if the gun was missing or not, at that point." He pauses, studying me with a reproving air. "You know it would be a mistake to try and cover for your husband, don't you?"

I stare at him, slack jawed. "That's not what—"

I break off at a sharp knock on the door. A second officer sticks his head inside, motioning for Price to step out of the room.

He heaves himself to his feet. "I'll leave you to stew on what I've said for a bit and then we'll take another crack at this."

The minute the door closes behind him, I press my fingers into my temples. This can't be happening. This is wrong—all wrong. I wipe the tears from my eyes and pull out my phone to send Cash another message. I stare pitifully at the screen, willing him to reply, but his response never comes. All my previous texts remain unanswered. My skin crawls as it occurs to me that they might have arrested him already. What if they're questioning him in the room next door? Maybe they're hoping I'll give them some incriminating piece of evidence so they can officially charge him. They're wasting their time. That's never going to happen. They're one-hundred percent wrong about Cash.

Minutes go by, without any sign of Price returning. My

eyes fall on the Manila folder on the other side of the desk. I glance up at the camera in the corner of the room. I'm guessing I'm not supposed to touch the file.

Then again, why would an experienced police officer have left it lying on the desk unless he wanted me to read it?

42

LEXI

Slowly, I stretch a finger out and place it on one corner of the folder. I slide it toward me an inch or two, then put my hands back in my lap, waiting to see what, if anything, will happen. I'm half-expecting the door to burst open like a scene from some dystopian movie, and a gaggle of helmeted officers to come rushing in and haul me off to some reeducation camp where I'll be forced to chant, *I must not touch the folder* from morning 'til night.

Maybe I'm the one who's going crazy.

I throw another furtive look up at the camera angled toward the table. No repercussions, so far. It's possible they don't monitor the cameras all the time. It's also possible they want me to open that file and see the evidence they've amassed against Cash. But he didn't do what they're insinuating, whatever they think that is—something bad, although, they still haven't spelled it out exactly. I'm afraid they're waiting for me to trip up and put a nail in his coffin. Maybe they even suspect me of trying to cover for him. Anger wells up inside me at the injustice of it all. I knew from the beginning that Price was utterly incompetent. That file will prove nothing. Anything in it can only be circum-stantial. But I need to warn Cash what Price is up to. I start composing a text to him and then delete it. What's the point? I've already sent him five or six urgent messages, maybe more, and he hasn't responded to any of them.

The silence in the room is overpowering. The whole outside world could have been abducted by aliens and I wouldn't know it. I'm starting to lose my mind in here. I almost wish Price would come back in to assure me I'm not the last human standing—almost. Truth be told, it's a relief to have some respite from watching him work his jowls as he formulates a question.

My eyes land on the manila folder once more. I feel like I'm in one of those research experiments where they leave young children in a room with a plate of cookies and a warning not to touch them, all in a bid to test their willpower, or propensity to lie, or some other such nonsense. What do they expect the kids to do when all other distractions have been removed from their surround-ings? It's a set-up—just like this is.

I glower across the table at the folder. I can't imagine I would be breaking any serious laws by taking a quick peek. It's not illegal to touch police property, is it? Do I have time to make a quick call and find out—a phone-a-friend, or ask-the-audience moment before Price returns and settles his silly-putty frame into the seat opposite me once more?

I throw a harried glance at the door before reaching for the file. This time I fully commit, spinning it around to face me and flipping it open. I promised myself I would fight for my husband, and that's exactly what I intend to do. My heart sinks when I see page after page of Price's laborious notes from reports, interviews, log sheets, and witness statements. I don't know where to begin, and I may have only seconds to peruse the file. An interview with Eleanor catches my eye, and I stop flicking pages to read what lies she's told Price about us. One section in particular stabs me in the gut: *Cash adores Jessica. He wants her back. He told me he regrets his hasty decision to marry Lexi.*

Price has underlined it and written *possible motive* with a question mark next to it. My face heats up. Eleanor is a barefaced liar! Cash tells me all the time how much he loves me and that I'm the best. Granted, he's never said we're soul-mates, which is how he described his relationship with Jess, but it's early days. Everyone knows sentiment grows over time.

I shrivel into my seat and cast an uneasy glance up at the camera lens trained on me. I'm tempted to rip out the page and shred Eleanor's lies, but that would do nothing to help Cash's cause. Price would be only too delighted to nail me with some trumped-up charge for destruction of property—in fact, he'd revel in it.

I grit my teeth and continue flicking haphazardly through the pages, stopping only to read what Price has highlighted or asterisked. I need to know if he has anything significant on Cash. As I scan through page after page of notes, my mood darkens. It's clear Price has been working hard to build a case against my husband. I knew I shouldn't have trusted him. His incompetence has sent him blundering down the wrong path. My heart flutters with fear when I turn to a page titled: *Character assessment.* My eyes travel slowly down the page.

- *Player.*
- *Dated Jess before divorce with Anya was finalized.*
- *Married Lexi after 5 months to make Jess jealous?*
- *Lexi unaware of meetings with Jess in Black Horse Tavern.*
- *Profile on Platinum Pairs online dating site.*

. . .

I CLENCH and unclench my fist, my loathing of Price increasing by the minute. I hate what I'm reading even more. On paper, I have to admit it looks bad. I didn't know Cash had started dating Jess before he and Anya were divorced—I only knew she had an affair and left him. And it's true I was unaware he was meeting Jess behind my back, at least, at first. Frowning in concentration, I flip to the next page.

Summary of interview with Helen Powers:

• *Claims Wade saw Cash and Jess Spicer together at the Black Horse Tavern on several occasions.*

• *Thinks Cash is a pathological liar.*

• *Says Lexi was traumatized after the knife attack and miscarriage. Naive and easily manipulated.*

• *Finds it suspicious that Cash discovered the gun was missing.*

• *Fears for Lexi's safety.*

I STARTLE at the sound of footsteps in the corridor. In one frantic sweep, I slap the folder closed and shove it back across the table. Almost immediately, I notice I forgot to turn it back around to face Price's seat. My heart is beating so loudly it's drowning out the footsteps. A moment later, I realize it's because they've faded out of earshot as someone walked on by the interview room. I place my palms on the desk and suck in a quick breath, my pulse slowly returning to normal. Several minutes go by before I pluck up the courage to reach across the table again for the file. I thumb through the pages until I find the place where I left off reading. My eyes bounce through random notes as my brain tries to piece together the information.

Follow up:

Jess Spicer's text: I wish she would disappear off the face of the earth. Did Cash promise to handle it for her?

Is Cash using vandalism/harassment to scare Lexi out of marriage? Had access to home and vehicle.

Cash insisted on buying a gun, despite Lexi's hesitation.

Lexi at hospital when Cash is shot at. No witnesses to his story.

Did Cash recruit Wade to help him?

What is Cash's relationship with his mother? Is he in cahoots with her?

Mila was picked up early from Eleanor's—was the fire staged?

Naomi says Cash was the last person to see Jess. Did she refuse his advances/attempt to get back with her?

I GRIMACE. It's all speculation, but I can see where Price is going with this. I leaf through a couple more pages until I come to a paper-clipped note titled: *warrants.*

Vehicle warrant: Lavender scarf discovered in Cash's car.

My eyes widen. It's news to me that they searched his car. They didn't impound it, unless they have it at the yard now—which would mean he's been arrested, as I suspected. My brain pounds against my skull as I consider this frightening twist.

Phone warrant: Deleted texts recovered.

That's odd. Cash told me Price never followed through on the warrant after his phone was smashed. My breathing grows shallow as I begin reading the first deleted text.

I made a terrible mistake marrying Lexi so quickly. I feel trapped. We're not on the same wavelength. Losing the baby made me realize my mother was right—that was the only reason I proposed in the first place. Guilt, I suppose, or a sense of responsibility. Please give me another chance, my darling Jess. Say you'll meet me at our special spot in the park tonight? Name the time and I'll be there.

I jerk upright when my phone pings in my purse. I rummage around for it, desperate to confront my husband. But when I pull it out, it's a message from the hospital.

I'm sorry to tell you that Helen Powers passed away a few minutes ago.

43

CASH

"Cash Reisinger, you have the right to remain silent ..."

I jump up from my desk, scattering the plans I was working on to the floor. A thick fog envelops my brain as the arresting officer rattles off my rights.

"Wait! This is a mistake!" I protest. "What's this about? I didn't do anything ..."

I cringe under the horrified looks my colleagues shoot my way as I begin the long walk of shame from my office on the third floor of the engineering firm where I work, to the elevator. Will stares at me, jaw askew, no doubt already scouring our lunch conversation the other day for some juicy tidbits to share with the office. My scrambled brain is fueled up by a toxic concoction of excessive caffein consumption and sleep deprivation. I can't make any sense of why they're arresting me. I need to call Lexi. Maybe I'm in the middle of a nightmare. The officer who cuffed me presses the elevator button and it jerks into action, instantly dispelling any lingering hope that I'm going to wake up in a minute.

After I'm booked in at the station, an officer escorts me to an interview room and removes my handcuffs. He closes the door behind him, leaving me alone with my muddled thoughts and a plastic cup of water as my only solace. I rest my elbows on the table and rub my wrists, trying to figure out how on earth I ended up here. I know Price has been investigating me, but what could he possibly have found? I have nothing to hide—well, not much, at any rate. I didn't abduct Jess—not that I haven't thought about it in a fleeting, nostalgic kind of way. I certainly didn't harm her. Apparently, that's not what it looks like from law enforcement's perspective.

I glance around the stark, stale room, taking in the lone camera watching me from above like a predator ready to swoop down and nab its vulnerable prey. Are they watching me now—trying to gauge my reactions for any indication of guilt? Are they going to leave me here to sweat for a few hours before they officially tell me why they brought me in? It's not like I don't know why they've arrested me. I'm their prime suspect in Jess's disappearance. They must have some compelling evidence to be confident enough to make an arrest at this point—but what? Have they found her?

I stare morosely at a random spot on the wall opposite me. This is Naomi's doing. She must have given them something incendiary. She told them I met with Jess the night she disappeared. But she's mistaken. It's true I wanted to—I might even have been tempted to run away with her if she had agreed to meet me. But it never happened. She didn't text me back until the next day, and by then, I'd come to regret sending the text in the first place. I furrow my brow as I think back to the disturbing message she sent me the following morning: *I wish she would disappear off the face of the earth.* I shudder even now at the vitriol spewing from it.

My head jerks up at the sound of the door opening. Price ambles into the room, his body jiggling as he trundles toward the metal table. It feels like the entire room quakes when he flops down in the chair opposite me. I wrinkle my nose at the objectionable odor of cigarette smoke trailing him.

"Why am I here?" I demand.

"You know why you're here," Price answers, placing a file folder on the table in front of him.

I stare blankly back at him. I feel like Winston in George Orwell's 1984, being pressured into confessing to some elusive thought crime.

"Is this about Jess?" I say, leaning forward with what I hope is an earnest and trustworthy expression on my face. "Because I had nothing to do with her disappearance. I have no idea where she is. You know she's been harassing me and my wife—you have a log of all our complaints. She's probably gone on the run. She could be in Mexico for all I know."

Price tents the tips of his fingers together and appraises me. "The fact remains that you were the last person to see her."

"No!" I slam my palms down hard on the table. "It's not true! I already told you I never met up with her. She didn't reply to my text. I stayed home all that night. You can ask my wife."

Price scratches his neck just above the sweat line on the collar of his shirt. "That's not a convincing alibi. We both know your wife would say anything to protect you."

I open my mouth to protest, then snap my lips shut. There's no sense in denying it. He's right. Lexi would do anything to keep me—even if it meant lying to a police officer. I opt for a different tack. "Look, I didn't do anything to

Jess. I'm the one who's in danger here. She shot out my window. My daughter could have been killed."

"But she wasn't. Remarkably, she wasn't even in the room with you when the shot was fired." Price traces a finger back and forth beneath the tip of his nose before flipping open the folder in front of him. "Ballistics has established that your gun was used in the incident. When did you report it stolen?"

I wrinkle my brow, trying to sort the past few days into some kind of coherent sequence. "It was ... Sunday. No! Monday. That's right. We had just ordered pizza."

Price eyes me skeptically. "And that's when you discovered the gun was missing."

"Yes. I went to get it out ... you know, just in case we needed it that evening. The safe was locked but the gun was gone."

"Right," Price says in a tone reeking of derision. "And who locked the gun in the safe to begin with?"

I squirm in my seat, increasingly uncomfortable with his line of questioning. "I did."

"*I did*, said the little red hen," Price mutters to himself, as he adds something to his notes.

I stare at him in disbelief. "Is this some kind of joke to you? Are you even taking this seriously? Why am I here?"

He twirls his pen between his fingers, pinning me with a heavy-lidded gaze. "Believe me, Mr. Reisinger, I'm taking this very seriously." He twists his lips into a sardonic grin. "*I made a terrible mistake. I feel trapped. Please give me another chance.*" He raises his brows. "I believe you were serious when you wrote that—deadly serious as a matter of fact."

44

CASH

I've been in custody now for close to six hours. They won't let me talk to Lexi, although they did allow me to call a lawyer. She enters the room I'm being questioned in wearing black pants, a cream-colored silk blouse, and three-inch heels. A gold bracelet jangles on her wrist when she extends a smooth olive-skinned hand to greet me. "Isabel Diaz," she says in a deep-throated voice, dispensing with the usual *pleased-to-meet-you* niceties. Maybe it's a good thing. I need someone who's more punch than show. It's slowly beginning to sink in that I'm in serious trouble.

Isabel pulls an iPad from a sleek leather briefcase and sets it down in front of her. "Now, let's start at the beginning."

I do my best to bring her up to speed on everything that's transpired. She stops me from time to time to clarify some of my statements when my emotions start to get the better of me, or I go off on a non-sequential tangent. When I run out of things to tell her, I lean back in my seat and rub the aching spot between my eyes. "Can you get me out of here? I don't want to spend the night. My wife must be sick with worry."

"Do you know if the police have questioned her, yet?" Isabel asks, scrutinizing me with intelligent, brown eyes.

I shake my head. "They haven't told me anything. Lexi knows I didn't do this. She'll vouch for me."

Isabel interlocks her fingers in front of her. "Spouses don't make for the most convincing witnesses. You'd be surprised how many people are willing to lie for their significant other, for any number of reasons—love, fear, insecurity. Even if she swears you never left the house the night Jess disappeared, it won't be enough. We can try pinging your phone—that would be one way to prove your whereabouts."

I wince. "That's the night I dropped it and smashed it."

Isabel taps on her iPad with a flawless, oval fingernail. "Based on what you've told me, it doesn't sound like the police have much to go on. I'll obtain copies of everything during discovery, of course. It would be a mistake to charge you when the only evidence they appear to have is circumstantial. Unless they obtain some direct evidence linking you to a crime, they'll have to release you within seventy-two hours."

"Seventy-two hours? I can't stay here that long." I rub my hand across my jaw. "What if Jess goes after Lexi while I'm locked up?"

"I'm sure your wife has been advised of the situation and can take appropriate steps to protect herself." Isabel offers a fleeting smile of condolence as she scrolls back through the notes she has taken. "Okay, I think we've covered everything. I'll let Price know we're ready for him now."

Ten minutes later, he trundles back into the room

brushing crumbs from his shirt—something flaky and nauseatingly sweet. I turn away from his penetrating gaze as he makes his way over to us. Isabel stands and introduces herself, giving Price's sweaty hand the briefest of shakes before dropping it like a hot potato. He places my file on the table in front of him. The chair opposite me creaks in protest as he resumes his seat.

"I've reviewed everything with my client, and it's clear he's been arrested purely on the basis of circumstantial evidence," Isabel begins. "In fact, nothing in the police report proves a crime has even been perpetrated against Mr. Reisinger's ex-girlfriend, Jessica Spicer."

Price licks his lips carefully, as though searching for stray crumbs, before responding. "As you well know, Ms. Diaz, when multiple pieces of circumstantial evidence are considered together, and they all point to the defendant's guilt—"

"Except they don't," Isabel interrupts. "Someone else could be responsible for Jessica's disappearance."

Price shifts his weight in the chair. "I'm afraid the evidence against Mr. Reisinger is ... considerable and convincing."

I shoot Isabel a worried look.

She leans back and crosses her legs. "I disagree with your analysis, unless some new evidence has come to light," she says, in a tone that suggests her patience is being taxed.

A faint smile dances on Price's lips. He likes this game. But it's not just a game to me. My freedom's at stake.

He presses his fingertips together. "We've located Jessica Spicer's car hidden under a pile of brush and branches in the woods."

My mouth falls open. "Is she ... okay?"

"Unlikely. Traces of blood and hair were found inside her vehicle." He heaves out an exaggerated sigh as he casually flips open the file folder he brought with him. "Are you ready to make a deal, now, Mr. Reisinger?"

45

LEXI

The timing couldn't be worse. I'm staring at my phone, digesting the news about Helen, while simultaneously reeling from Cash's *terrible mistake* that left him feeling trapped, as he put it, when the door is suddenly flung open and Price plods back into the room. My eyes swivel to the file folder lying open in front of me. A chill snakes down my spine. Price's face remains emotionless as he resumes his seat. He places a pudgy finger on the file and turns it around to face him in a slow, deliberate arc. "So, now that you know what your husband is up against, are you ready to cooperate?"

It takes all my willpower not to slap the smug smile off his face as I ask through gritted teeth, "Where is my husband?"

Price leafs nonchalantly through the pages in front of him. "He's here. He's been arrested."

"I want to see him," I say, half-rising out of my seat.

"I'm afraid that's not possible at the moment. He's with his lawyer."

"Lawyer? But ... he didn't do anything," I say, my voice wavering, a note of desperation creeping in.

"Mrs. Reisinger, Lexi, all indications are that your husband and Jessica Spicer were having an affair. We believe he was plotting with her to get rid of you."

"No! That's not true! He loves me ... he ... " My voice trails off. Do I know that for sure? I know he tried to love me. He wanted to. But he didn't love me like he loved her. *I made a terrible mistake ... my darling Jess.* He loved me out of guilt, out of a sense of responsibility—for the baby's sake.

Price taps his pen on the table. "It's possible Jessica had changed her mind about following through with the plan. Maybe she even tried to end the affair, and that's when your husband killed her."

"He did not kill her!" I yell. "You don't know him like I do. This is all her doing. She's trying to set him up. She's behind everything—"

"Yes, I know that's what you believe. I've heard it all before," Price says, flapping a hand dismissively. "But you have no proof. Our theory is that your husband shot at himself and tried to pin it on Jess."

"No! You've got it all wrong! It was her! She even sent him a picture of the gun she stole from our safe. What more proof do you want? Anya and Eleanor are in on it too—we have evidence of their involvement. They want me out of Cash's life, and they'll keep this up until he complies."

Price gives a dubious shake of his head. "Everything about Jess's disappearance points to foul play. Have you considered the possibility that Eleanor and Anya could be covering up for your husband? Don't you find it odd that your mother-in-law and her ex-daughter-in-law are suddenly thick as thieves after hating each other for years?"

I squeeze my hands in my lap, eying him warily. "My

husband is innocent. If they're covering for anyone, it's each other."

Price strokes a finger back and forth over his double chin as he thinks. "Perhaps you can help us prove it."

I blink, momentarily taken aback at this sudden change in course. "How?"

He studies me, hooded eyes unblinking. "Reach out to Cash's ex-wife. See if you can find out what happened to Jess." He leans across the table, a sober expression in his eyes. "You do want to prove your husband's innocence, don't you? You might be the only hope he has of remaining a free man."

LEXI

I'm under strict instructions not to tell Cash what I'm up to. Not that they've given me any opportunity to relay anything to him—he's still in police custody, his every word monitored. His lawyer says they have the right to hold him for up to seventy-two hours without charging him, which doesn't give me a whole lot of time to prove he's innocent.

When I arrive home, I glance across at the empty porch where Helen used to sit in her rocker. It's such a shame what happened to her—I wish it could have been Wade who died instead of her. I miss her, even though it's partly thanks to her that Cash has been arrested as a suspect in Jess's disappearance. I tried my best to allay her suspicions, explaining that she didn't know Cash like I did, but she kept insisting I was blinded by love. She always did try and look out for me.

I fix myself a grilled cheese sandwich, take a bite, then toss it in the trash. I really should eat something, but my stomach is a writhing mass of anxiety, and I don't think I can keep anything down. I retrieve my phone from my purse and pull up Anya's name in my contacts. Price suggested I reach out to her and Eleanor on the pretext of telling them about Cash being arrested. I chew on my lip as I consider the best course of action. If I text or call, the likelihood is they'll just ignore me.

After giving it some thought, I decide to drive over to Eleanor's instead. Maybe I can get Anya on her own for a few minutes and make my case to her—convince her it won't benefit her financially if Cash is behind bars. That should get her attention. It's not entirely the way Price wants me to do things, but he doesn't know my husband's exes like I do, and I have to think on my feet. At all costs, I have to get Cash out of this mess he's in before the case goes to trial. My hands are sweating as I grip the steering wheel and run through in my head what I need to relay. The hardest part will be getting rid of Eleanor long enough to have a private word with Anya. My mother-in-law always needs to feel like she's exerting control over every situation. But it hasn't worked out so well for her, of late. I imagine she's hating every minute of her required community service.

I park a couple of doors down from her house to make sure there's no chance of alerting her or Anya to my presence ahead of time. I ring the doorbell and practice pulling my lips into a disarming smile.

A moment later, the front door opens and Anya stares at me with a forbidding expression. Mila peeks out from behind her skirt, her thumb jammed into her mouth. I wiggle my fingers at her, and she smiles back shyly.

"What are you doing here?" Anya hisses, glancing up and down the street—presumably, searching for Cash.

"Is Eleanor home?"

"No," Anya snaps, attempting to close the door in my face.

I quickly wedge my foot in the frame. "Good. It's you I wanted to speak with. Can we talk inside?"

She folds her arms in front of her enhanced chest. Cash told me it was a gift from Anton on their first anniversary. A gift *for* Anton, more like it. Bet she wishes she could cash it in now for a deposit on an apartment instead of having to crash at her ex-mother-in-law's place. "Anything you have to say, you can say right where you're at. And if you're here to plead Cash's case, forget it. I'm petitioning the court for full custody. End of story."

"I'm not interested in getting in the middle of your custody spat, but I am here about Cash." I gesture discreetly to Mila. "We should talk in private."

Anya presses her lips tightly together, then grudgingly steps aside and gestures for me to come in. "I can give you five minutes. Eleanor's off doing her community service. She won't be happy to hear you stopped by."

"Don't tell her," I say with a shrug.

"Honey, you can go play on your iPad in your room for a few minutes," Anya says, shooing a delighted Mila off down the hall.

I follow Anya into the family room—a hideously decorated space crammed with every piece of glassware and China Eleanor has ever inherited, collected, or rummaged for in the estate sales she delights in frequenting. I doubt Mila is even allowed in here.

Anya throws herself into an uncomfortable, tufted wingback chair and sweeps a disgruntled look around the room. "Anton's decorator would have a fit if he could see where I'm living now. Eleanor has no taste whatsoever."

"I bet Anton's place was really something," I say, trying to look suitably awestruck at the prospect of enduring several minutes of nauseating descriptions of Cantera stone patios, the stunning—*simply stunning*—infinity pool, and the immense master suite complete with its own utterly superfluous kitchenette and sitting room. I give her what I consider a generous amount of time before interrupting her. It's nothing I haven't heard before ad nauseam. "Anya, the reason I'm here is to tell you that Cash has been arrested."

Her false eyelashes twitch a time or two as she comes down off the high of luxury living to the mundane topic of the father of her child. "That's just great! I hit him up for more money and he goes and gets himself locked up. What happened? Did he get a DUI, or something?"

I wet my lips and lean forward on the green velvet loveseat I'm perched on the edge of. "He's been arrested in connection with Jess's disappearance."

Anya's practiced pout falls apart. She stares at me, aghast, her snow-white veneers frozen in time.

I paint an equally woebegone expression on my face. "Of course, he won't be able to have Mila anymore if he doesn't make bail. And the trial will cost a fortune. He's already retained a lawyer, and she looks like the expensive type." I sigh heavily. "I really don't know what to do. He's innocent, of course, but proving it could bankrupt us."

Anya chews on her overblown lips, then jumps to her feet. "I could use a stiff drink. Want one?"

"Sure," I say, trying not to look euphoric when she trots off to the kitchen, leaving her phone peeking out from beneath the seat cushion.

47

LEXI

When I'm finished with Anya's phone, I resume my seat and pretend to be engrossed in a coffee table book on antiquing when she walks back in with our drinks.

She arches a brow at me. "Vodka tonic, will that work?"

"Perfect, thank you,' I say, reaching for the glass she hands me. I barely wet my lips before setting it down on the end table next to me. I have no intention of drinking it. I need to keep my wits about me and play this right because, as Price correctly pointed out, I really do want to prove my husband's innocence.

"So," Anya begins, carefully placing her glass on one of Eleanor's hideous medieval cat coasters. "What exactly are they saying Cash did?"

"They're being evasive. They haven't officially charged him with anything, yet, but it's clear Price thinks he had something to do with Jess's disappearance. Jess's sister told the police Cash was the last one to see her before she disappeared. They've found her car in the woods, and traces of her blood." I hesitate, unwilling to admit to what else they found inside it. "I think they're working on the assumption she's dead."

Anya swallows a huge gulp of her vodka tonic. "Yikes! I mean, I can see Cash confronting Jess, but murder … I'm not buying it."

"I'm with you. There's no way Cash killed her." I lean forward in my chair. "To be honest, I think she's setting him up. And someone's got to be helping her."

Anya frowns. "Like who?"

I shift uneasily in my seat. "Eleanor."

Anya throws back her head and lets out a scoffing laugh. "Not likely. That woman worships the ground her son walks on. She made my life miserable for the entire two years I was married to him. She was over the moon when I told her I'd filed for divorce a week after Mila was born."

"Exactly! She doesn't want him to be with me either." I scoot closer to the edge of my seat, closing the gap between us. "That's why she's doing this, Anya. To punish him! She knows the charges will never stick because there is no crime —Jess isn't dead."

"Why are you telling me this?" Anya asks, stroking her finger over a forehead that no longer creases.

I blow out a heavy breath. "I need your help to prove Cash's innocence. We both have a vested interest in getting him out of this mess. If he loses his job over these charges, you can kiss your child support goodbye."

Anya sips her drink, studying me over the rim of her glass. "What do you want me to do?"

"Persuade Eleanor to tell you where Jess is. She must be hiding her somewhere. We know she's still in the area because she trashed my car and broke into our house the other night." I bite my lip for a moment. "By the way, Cash thinks that might have been you. He thinks you're in on everything—that you're doing Eleanor's bidding in exchange for her paying your way."

"What? No! That's nonsense." Anya clutches her almost empty glass with an air of desperation. "I didn't even know Eleanor was helping Jess. I haven't seen or heard anything that would indicate she is."

"That's because you haven't been looking," I counter. "But you have the perfect opportunity now that you're living here. You could check her computer—find out if she's been in contact with Jess."

Anya widens her eyes. "How am I supposed to do that? I'm not a hacker."

"I have her passwords," I say casually, trying not to look ecstatic that she's buying into the idea of helping me. "Cash set them up for her." I take a shallow breath before moving to close the deal. "What do you say?"

Anya drains her drink and sets the cut glass tumbler down with a thunk. "I don't owe that witch a thing. Count me in."

48

CASH

The deal looks nothing like I expected it to. They've released me, for now, but instead of feeling jubilant, I feel hollow inside. I pace up and down the street in front of the police station like a caged animal with my newly installed ankle monitor. I don't want to go home and try acting like everything's normal when my heart has just imploded. I can't pretend in front of everyone—Lexi, my mom, Anya. How can I carry on as usual when Price is telling me Jess is dead? I still can't comprehend it. How could someone so vibrant be cut down in her prime and left to rot in some unmarked grave—or wherever it is they left her? Price told me they found more than just a few drops of blood in her car—enough to indicate she'd probably bled out. *Probably*. That word's like a defective flotation device but I cling to it, regardless. I know Jess would have fought for her life. There's a chance she might have survived the attack and is lying injured in the woods somewhere. Maybe a lone hunter who also happens to be a doctor will stumble across her and save her life. You hear about these kinds of miraculous stories from time to time. It isn't beyond the realm of possibility.

My heart starts to race as the Uber I ordered comes into view. Waves of panic crash over me. I can't do this! I don't know what I was thinking by agreeing to something so preposterous. I should go back inside and tell Price I've made a mistake. I want to retract the deal. But then what? He was adamant that without my cooperation Jess's killer might evade justice. I need to help him nail this case closed. What he did to me was brutal—arresting me and interrogating me like a criminal. But he had to be sure I wasn't involved in any way. So now, I have to put my head down and get on with this performance. Say nothing to anyone. This is my burden to bear—the price I must pay for loving Jess for far too long. I brought her into my marriage in a way I shouldn't have. I married Lexi knowing full well my heart was taken.

After the annoyingly cheerful Uber driver makes a third attempt to start up a conversation, I pull out my phone and stare conspicuously at the screen, tapping purposelessly. He eyes me in the rearview mirror, weighing the expression on my face before abandoning any further attempts to jaw for the entire fifteen-minute ride home. *Home.* The word fills me with dread. How can I look Lexi in the face and lie to her? Won't she see straight through me? And what about my mother? No doubt, she'll show up at the house the minute she hears I've been released on bail—at least, that's what Price wants me to tell everyone. Mom will want to seize control of the situation, hire a team of expensive lawyers, sue the police department—a tornado of vengeance, as always. She would lay down her life for me, but at what cost? I will never forgive her for constantly stoking the fire that burned everything I ever loved in the end.

The Uber pulls up outside my house and I climb out like an eighty-year-old, crippled by the weight of the task ahead of me. A shiver runs up my spine when I see Helen's house next door shrouded in darkness. *Someone pushed me.* I have a horrible feeling her death is connected to Jess's disappearance. But how can I prove it? As I make my way to my front door, I notice a light on in the converted garage in Helen's back yard. Price is convinced the killer acted alone, but I'm not so sure.

I'm tempted to knock on Wade's door, take him by the scruff of the neck, and make him tell me everything. The Black Horse Tavern is a far cry from the kind of drinking hole Wade ordinarily hangs out at. I suspect he followed me there. Did someone pay him to spy on me?

49

CASH

The minute I walk into the kitchen, Lexi jumps up screaming from the table and throws her arms around my neck. "Cash! I can't believe you're home. Why didn't you call me? I would have come and picked you up."

"I didn't want you leaving the house alone at night. It's too dangerous." I say, untangling myself from her grip and slumping down in a chair. "Is the back door locked?"

She nods. "Yes. What did Price—"

"Have you seen Wade at all since he got back?" I interrupt, peering out through the kitchen window at the dimly lit unit in the yard next door.

"I ... uh. No. He's been holed up inside the whole time."

I didn't miss the note of hesitation. Is she lying to me? Has she seen him—spoken to him? "You need to stay away from Wade. He's more dangerous than you realize."

"Cash, what did Price say? Why did they release you? Does this mean you're no longer a suspect?"

I dig my hands through my hair, so she won't be able to

read the lie on my face. "I'm out on bail, thanks to my expensive lawyer."

"Bail!" Lexi's face crumples. "What are they charging you with?"

"It's bad." I take a raspy breath. "Second-degree murder."

She brings her brows together. "But ... how can they? They have no body. They can't even prove she's dead. We can prove she's alive!"

I glance over at her with a flicker of hope, despite everything I know to be true. "How?"

"She's still harassing us, for one thing."

I instantly deflate. "We've been over this a million times. We don't know for sure if it's her."

Lexi pulls at the sleeve of her sweater. "I'm working on something. Price has asked for my help."

I frown across at her. "What do you mean?"

Lexi sighs. "You're not going to like it, but Price agrees with my theory that Eleanor might have orchestrated everything. He thinks Jess was helping her, but wanted out when things took a dangerous turn. He suspects Eleanor did something to her and Anya might be helping cover things up. She's beholden to Eleanor now that she's living in her house, but she also doesn't want you to end up in prison, leaving her trapped and penniless. Price asked me to reach out to Anya and see if I can find out anything that would prove your innocence."

I rub my jaw, digesting her plan. "And will you ... reach out to her?"

"I already did. I went over earlier this evening and talked to her. She's going to root around on your mom's computer and try and find out if she's been communicating with Jess." Lexi hesitates. "I gave her your mom's passwords. I hope that's okay."

I lean back in my chair and sling my arm over it. "I'm pretty sure that's illegal. You should have talked this over with me first. I can't risk getting into any more trouble than I'm already in."

"I know it can't be easy hearing that Price suspects your own mother of masterminding everything, but if we can prove Jess is alive, it means you won't be going to jail for something you didn't do."

I nod distractedly, suddenly overwhelmed by everything that's gone down in the last twenty-four hours, and the stomach-dropping emotional rollercoaster I've been on for weeks on end. I've gone from speculating that Jess was abducted by Wade, to thinking she might be hiding out in a cabin in the woods somewhere, then fearing she was imprisoned in my mother's basement, to facing the very real possibility that she's dead. I'm so numb inside right now, I'm not sure I'll ever be able to feel anything again.

"Are you hungry?" Lexi asks, getting to her feet. "I can make you a chicken Panini."

"Sure. That would be great." I tweak a smile of thanks. Even the thought of eating makes my stomach seethe, but I need a few minutes of peace so I can sift through the thoughts flapping maniacally around inside my head. I wish there was another way forward, but if there is, I can't see it. I grit my teeth and get to my feet, committed to the course I'm on.

Ankle monitor or not, it's time I paid Wade another visit.

50

LEXI

Anya calls me back the following morning. "I found something," she says, her voice low and urgent. "Can you meet me in town? We can't talk here."

My stomach tightens. "Sure. How about the Starbucks in the mall? I can be there an hour from now. I don't start work until noon."

The place is packed as usual, but I manage to nab a high-top table at the back. I shift impatiently in my plastic seat as I wait for Anya to show up. She's running fifteen minutes late and I'm starting to think she might have bailed on me. Or worse, what if Eleanor's discovered what she's up to? I pick nervously at the skin on my thumb until it starts to bleed. The Starbucks employee wiping down the tables directs increasingly more pointed stares my way. Maybe I should go ahead and order a drink. As I check my phone for the umpteenth time for a message from Anya, she suddenly slides into the chair opposite me.

"Sorry, I'm late," she pants. "Eleanor wouldn't stop talking about Cash's arrest, and how humiliating the whole thing was for her. I didn't tell her he's out on bail—figured that was his call."

I give an approving nod. "She doesn't know you're meeting me, does she?"

"Are you kidding me? She'd have a fit. I told her I had a doctor's appointment."

"Good," I say, rising to my feet. "I'll get the drinks. What are you having?"

When I return to the table with two vanilla lattes, Anya pulls out a folded sheet of paper and passes it to me with shaking fingers.

"What's this?" I ask, setting my drink to one side.

"An email from Jess." Anya leans toward me and lowers her voice. "You were right. She's alive and well, and Eleanor is helping her."

I open up the page and begin reading.

Things are working out so much better than I could ever have imagined. The police are convinced I must have been mortally wounded. I had my doubts, but I guess that bag of blood my sister drew did the trick! Hopefully, Cash will have learned his lesson and appreciate us both a whole lot more once this is over and done with. I'll lie low for a couple more days. Just make sure and tie up those loose ends so everything points to Anya.

"Can you believe it?" Anya hisses when I look up. "They were going to try and pin everything on me. All this time, I thought Eleanor actually wanted to try and patch things up with me for Mila's sake. The only reason she took me in was so she could set me up as the fall person for her sick scheme."

I shake my head slowly, scanning the words in front of me once more. "I'm so sorry, Anya. I guess she truly hates anyone who comes between her and her son."

"Except for Jess," Anya fumes.

"It's only a matter of time before she turns on her too," I say grimly.

Anya cocks her head to one side. "You think so?"

I let out a snort. "She knows too much."

"You don't think Eleanor will harm her, do you?" Anya asks.

My chest heaves up and down as I weigh my words carefully. "I guess we'll find out if she doesn't reappear."

51

LEXI

It took some doing, but I finally manage to persuade Anya to accompany me to the police station to show Price the email she found on Eleanor's computer. She was afraid she would be implicated in the plot, but I assured her that Price already has Eleanor firmly in his crosshairs. Cash advised us not to mention the fact that Anya hacked into the computer, so we opted instead to say Eleanor left it on and Anya saw the email when she went to print out something.

"I'll drive," Anya says. "If we run late, I can pick Mila up from school on the way back."

Price keeps us waiting for a good thirty minutes before ushering us into his office. "What can I do for you, ladies?" he asks, his expression unreadable as he heaves himself into his chair.

"I did what you suggested and reached out to Anya," I say. "She's found something she thinks will prove Cash's innocence." I nod to her, and she fumbles in her Bottega Veneta tote for the email.

Price studies the page she hands him.

"It was sent yesterday," she says, with a tremor in her voice. "This proves Jess is alive and she's been scheming with Eleanor all along."

"If it's genuine, it would certainly clear Cash of any wrongdoing," Price acknowledges.

"So you'll drop the charges?" I blurt out.

He raises a hand. "Not so fast. We'll bring Naomi in for questioning first. If she participated in medical fraud like this email is claiming, then her nursing career is over. That reality might be enough to shake the truth out of her."

"They're going to try and pin everything on me," Anya says, tracing her fingers nervously over her brow.

Price presses his lips together. "I'm not sure what they've planned next, but you need to remain vigilant. You could be in danger. Is there anywhere else you can stay in the meantime, a hotel, perhaps?"

Anya flushes. "I'm in the process of a divorce so money is tight. I could stay with my sister, but she lives two hours from here and I don't want to have to pull Mila out of school with only a few weeks left in the term."

I tug at my sleeve before glancing sheepishly at Anya. "You can stay with us, if you want. It would be good for Mila to see more of her dad."

Anya stares at me, mouth agape. "I … don't know what to say. That's extremely generous of you."

I shrug. "It's Mila's home too. She needs both her parents around."

"What am I going to tell Eleanor?" Anya asks.

"Tell her you and Cash need to work out some custody and child support issues in the event he ends up going to prison," I suggest. "He's not allowed to leave the house with his ankle monitor, so it would be easier if you stayed with us for a couple of days."

Price gives an approving nod. "That should work."

Anya presses her fingertips to her temples. "I feel nervous for Jess. What if Eleanor turns against her, too? I'm afraid of what she might do to her."

Price shoots me a knowing look. "We can't warn her or protect her unless she comes forward." He places the email evidence from Eleanor's computer inside the Manila folder in front of him and gets to his feet. "If you get any leads on where she is, let me know."

Anya is unusually quiet on the drive back to Eleanor's to pack up her stuff, gripping the steering wheel with both hands and staring directly ahead.

"Are you okay?" I ask. "Don't worry. She won't be able to hurt you. I'll be right there with you."

"It's not me I'm worried about. It's Jess. I actually really like her. She has such charisma about her. I thought she was good for Cash."

I clench my teeth until they hurt. Here we go again. Charming, gregarious, intelligent, kind-hearted, and all-sorts-of-other-admirable-words everyone gushes over Jess. It seems no one can get enough of her.

Anya glances over at me apologetically. "It's not that you aren't good for him. It's just ... well, anyway I always thought he and Jess would go the distance. Between you and me, I think Eleanor scared her off. And then Jess regretted it. They both regretted it."

I paste a polite smile over the snarl threatening to erupt on my lips. That's when I decide Anya must die too.

52

CASH

"We're getting close to making an arrest," Price tells me over the phone.

"Have you ... found her?" I stammer, scrunching my eyes shut at the thought of Jess lying beneath the leaves in the forest somewhere, her lifeless body swarming with insects fixing to take up abode.

"Not yet. But I think we have what we need to make the charges stick. The email was sent to your mother through a VPN server, just like the others, purportedly from Jess—all fabricated of course. Can you come down to the station? I'd like to verify some things with you and prepare you for what comes next. We'll remove your ankle monitor too."

I rub my wrists as I take a seat in Price's office, wondering how Lexi will feel once the handcuffs are on her. I hope they arrest her in a public place so she can feel some of the humiliation I endured. I can't even begin to comprehend what she's done. Every time I think about it, my head starts spinning so fast I think I'm going to pass out.

"Coffee?" Price asks, leaning his head around the door.

"Sure, thanks," I say. I won't drink it, but I need something to do with my hands. The minute I stop fidgeting, I start hyperventilating. It feels like I'm dying. I still can't fathom the enormity of the situation. I have so many unanswered questions, it seems like I'm losing my mind. Everything I try to grasp about my life—what I thought was my life—disintegrates beneath the weight of Lexi's lies. Everything other than the fact that she loved me, except that her concept of love is a dark, obsessive triad forged from lust, jealousy, and wrath.

She knew she wanted me from the first day she set eyes on me in The Steamed Bean. And she made sure she got what she wanted by surreptitiously slipping my wallet out of my back pocket so she could step in and save the day. Fool that I was, I fell for it. Who doesn't love a hero? I was nursing a broken heart at the time, and she was only too ready to administer the salve I needed to heal—sweet, gentle, caring, kind Lexi. Until she wasn't. Maybe something broke inside her when she realized I was still in love with Jess, or maybe she was always that way and managed to keep it hidden beneath a mask of normalcy.

More details are coming to light all the time. Yesterday, Price spoke to an ex-boyfriend of Lexi's who told him she faked having cancer to stop him from leaving her. He hung in there for several months, even shaving his head in solidarity, until his sister, who had picked up on some inconsistencies, called the clinic where Lexi claimed to be undergoing chemotherapy, and exposed her lies. Oddly enough, it made me feel marginally better to know I wasn't the only doofus who'd been played for a fool.

It never occurred to me there was a possibility Lexi wasn't pregnant. It looked like the real deal to me, as far as I remembered from when Anya was pregnant with Mila. She was in the bathroom throwing up, browsing baby websites, buying maternity clothes—she even had an ultrasound photo—clipped from Google, as it turned out.

"Here you go," Price says, plonking down a Styrofoam cup in front of me.

I curl my fingers around it and mumble my thanks.

Price flips open the manila folder in front of him—the real case file, not the one he fabricated for Lexi's benefit. He may look like a tortoise, but behind those sleepy eyes presides a sharp intellect.

"You said you were getting close to making an arrest," I say. "Did some new evidence come to light?"

Price gives a curt nod. "We tracked down the druggie kid she hired to spray paint your wall. He also opened up your garage and set up the sign offering your stuff for free. We pressed him on the arson, but he denies setting fire to your mother's house. Lexi paid him in cash so there's no paper trail, but he was only too happy to give us a statement once we reeled off all the potential charges he could be facing."

"I suppose he threw the bleach on Lexi's clothes too," I say.

"He swears he never went inside your house. My guess is she did it herself before you left for your mother's that night."

I nod dismally. "Makes sense. Something snapped in her after Jess stopped by the house to pick up her iPad. That's when everything started happening. She was bound and determined to make me hate Jess. It wasn't enough that we were no longer together." I stare down at the floor, trying to imagine what I could have done differently. Would it have made any difference if I had been honest with Lexi from the start—told her I wasn't ready to date, that I was still in love with Jess? That, deep down, I regretted breaking up with her and secretly hoped she would come back to me.

I groan and rub my hands over my face. "All this time, I thought Jess was the evil genius. It blows my mind how deviously Lexi operated in plain sight. All those cards, and emails from various servers, messages from burner phones —how did she do it? One time we were even watching a movie together when both our phones blew up with a text at the same time."

Price throws me a pitying look. "There's an App for everything these days. She could have used one that allows you to send delayed messages. That way, she was sitting innocently by your side, when the message came through."

He shuffles some papers in front of him. "I'll arrange for police protection—undercover officers—for your mother, Anya, and your daughter until we can move in and make an arrest."

"How much longer is it going to take? You still haven't found Jess's body. Are you going to wait until she kills someone else?"

"No. We can try her for murder without a body. We just have to make sure we nail down all the loose ends in terms of evidence. I've already dispatched officers to the store where she works to arrest her the minute she shows up to start her shift. Until we have her in custody, you need to be aware that the other members of your family that she's been making scapegoats of are also at risk."

I grit my teeth. "I bet she planted those notecards when we went to Mom's for dinner that night. All this time, I was furious at my mother for sending the card and destroying Lexi's wedding dress." I let out a disgruntled snort. "She didn't tamper with her muffins either—I sent some off to be analyzed. I'm guessing Lexi put something in the tea she gave me to wash them down with."

The door opens and an officer signals to Price to step outside. Several minutes go by before he returns with a grave look on his face.

"It appears we're too late. Anya's at the hospital. Your mother found her lying at the bottom of the stairs."

53

CASH

I leap up out of my chair, my heart halfway up my throat. "What happened? Is Mila okay?"

"Your mother's on her way to pick her up from school right now," Price replies.

"And Anya?"

"She's conscious. You can ride in the squad car with me."

I'm sick to my stomach with worry by the time we arrive at the hospital—a record six minutes later, thanks to Price activating his lights.

The ER doctor gives us a brief overview of Anya's condition before allowing us into her room to speak with her. "We're prepping her for surgery. She has two broken legs and a fractured wrist. Fortunately for her, the MRI didn't indicate any bleeding on the brain." He nods and gestures for us to go in.

A nurse, busy adjusting a drip line, raises her brows when she spots Price and then exits the room briskly. Anya slowly turns her head to look at us. I suck in a sharp breath, aghast at how swollen her face is—not something the doctor prepared us for. "Anya, I'm so sorry," I say, moving to her side and reaching for her hand. "What happened?"

She frowns, blinking as though trying to gather her thoughts. "I ... was helping Lexi." She throws me a woebegone look. "We knew you didn't hurt Jess. We were trying to prove it." She turns to look at Price. "Lexi suggested we look through Eleanor's bedroom while she was doing her community service hours—in case she was hiding the gun."

She falls silent and closes her eyes, a pained expression on her face.

"What happened next?" Price prompts.

She lets out a soft, fluttering sigh. "I followed Lexi upstairs, and she tripped at the top and fell back against me. Next thing I know, I'm tumbling. I ... I knocked myself out. Lexi must have called for an ambulance. When I came to, I was already at the hospital." She blinks around the room. "Where is she? Is she okay?"

I lock eyes with Price, and he gives a tight shake of his head. There will be plenty of time later to explain everything—but not now, right when she's about to go into surgery. "She's fine," I tell her.

Anya grasps my arm feebly. "Where's Mila? Does she know?"

"Mom's on her way to pick her up from school. They'll be here shortly. You'll see her when you get out of surgery."

Anya's grip tightens. "I don't want Mila staying with your mother. She's dangerous. She's been helping Jess this whole time. Promise me you'll take Mila home with you and Lexi."

I swallow hard. "Don't worry, I'll make sure Mila is with me at all times."

Anya smiles and releases me before closing her eyes again. "Thank you, Cash. You were always a good dad."

I grimace. *Not such a good husband.*

An orderly enters the room and reaches for the clipboard. "Okay, are we ready, Anya?"

I wave encouragingly at her as she's whisked off down the corridor and through the double doors to surgery.

"Sounds to me like Lexi tried to kill her," Price mutters. "The only reason your ex-wife's not dead is because your mother came home early. Lexi must have heard her car pull up outside and ran out the back of the house."

My blood runs cold. "Are you saying she hasn't been apprehended yet?"

Price shakes his head. "My officers were in position. She never showed up for work."

54

CASH

"I dispatched officers to your house, too, but Lexi hasn't shown up there either," Price says.

My throat feels like it's closing over. "Mila!" I gasp. "Why is my mother not here yet?"

Price frowns, reaches for his radio and steps outside.

I snatch up my phone and dial my mother's number, pacing frantically as I wait for her to pick up.

"Cash! I must admit I'm surprised to hear from—"

"Never mind that! Is Mila with you?"

"I'm just pulling into the school parking lot right now," she says, in an injured tone. "There was an accident on ninth and the traffic was all backed up."

"Stay on the line. Put Mila on as soon as you have her in the car."

"Really, Cash. Do you have to be so impatient? I'm exiting the car as we speak. Perhaps it would be better if I broke the news to Mila about her mother's fall."

"Just get a move on!" I yell.

She tuts her displeasure. "There's no need to be rude.

That wretched woman has been such a bad influence on you."

If only you knew. I force myself to breathe slowly in and out. For once in our lives, we're in agreement about something.

"How's Anya doing?" my mother asks.

"She's in surgery, multiple broken bones. Thankfully, no head injury."

"That's a relief. She was out cold when I found her at the bottom of the stairs ... oh, hello there, Mrs. Sutton!" Just like that, I'm dropped from the conversation. I try to curb my impatience as she and Mrs. Sutton exchange pleasantries.

My mind is running in a thousand different directions at once as I try to decipher what's happening on the other end of the line. I can hear my mother greeting someone else as she walks up to the school office—the custodian, perhaps? Or another parent picking a child up early for a doctor's appointment? A door clangs and I hear a muffled exchange, presumably with the school secretary.

After several agonizing minutes, I can stand it no longer. "Mom, are you there?" I raise my voice and try again. "Mom!"

"Yes, I'm here, son. Just give me a minute, *please*! There's a sign-out process I have to follow."

I drag a hand through my hair in frustration as she resumes her conversation. Why is she wasting time chitchatting with the secretary when Anya's in surgery and my daughter's life could be at stake?

Price strides back into the room. "I have officers en route to the school. They'll escort your mother and Mila from there."

"I'm on the phone with Mom right now. She just got there."

"Tell her to stay put until the police arrive. I'll have them accompany her and Mila to a safe location until we've apprehended Lexi."

I nod distractedly, wondering how long it takes a six-year-old to pack up her backpack and put on her coat.

My heart leaps in my chest when my mother's voice comes on the line again. "Cash? Are you still there?"

"Yes, Of course I'm here! What's taking so long?"

"There seems to be some kind of misunderstanding. Oh, wait just a minute. The secretary's mouthing something at me."

Before I can stop her, she's left me hanging again.

Price raises enquiring brows and I roll my eyes at him. "She's talking to the school secretary. Apparently, it takes an Act of Congress to get a six-year-old out of class."

"Cash, are you—"

"Yes! I'm here! What's going on?"

"It seems Mila has been picked up already. You might have told me you were going to ask Lexi to get her. If I'd known that, I could have saved myself the grief of sitting in all that traffic. Cash? Are you listening?"

"Yes," I croak into the phone. I sink down on the edge of the bed and lock eyes with Price. "Lexi has my daughter."

55

"I'm not s'posed to ride in the car without my booster seat," Mila says, eying me dubiously as I plug in her seatbelt.

"I know. Silly Mommy forgot to give it to me," I say in a sing-song voice as I slide in behind the wheel and pull my baseball cap down over my eyes.

Mila giggles, and kicks the back of my seat, making me flinch. I grit my teeth, forcing a smile at her in the rearview mirror to hide the fact that what I'd really like to do to her is —*No!* I can't allow myself to go there. I promised myself I wouldn't harm the child. She's not the problem. Mila is most certainly not the problem—she's the solution, I remind myself. As long as I have Cash's daughter, he'll do exactly what I want. I just need to take my time and make small, calculated moves, each of which will bring me one step closer to my goal.

"Can we get ice cream, Lexi?" Mila asks.

"Hmm," I say, pretending to think. "That's a great idea. But first, you need to drink something. Mommy wants you to stay hydrated. There's some juice in your flask in the cup holder."

"Is it apple juice? 'Cause I only like apple juice. Not any other juice."

I grimace inwardly. "I'm not sure what Mommy put in there, but you need to drink it up if you want to get ice cream."

Mila lets out an exasperated sigh. "O-kay."

I watch as she leans forward, struggling to reach her flask, her fingertips barely grazing it.

I scoop it up and toss it in her lap. "There you go. Hurry up and drink it!"

She raises it to her face, then spots something out of the window that grabs her attention, the flask hovering maddeningly close to her lips.

I squeeze the steering wheel beneath my fingers, imagining for a flicker of a second it's her tiny throat. *No! Stop it, Lexi!* I gasp out loud, realizing just in time that I'm swerving into the adjacent lane. Shaking, I give a feeble wave of acknowledgment to the driver glowering across at me as he pulls ahead. I take a shallow breath and glance in the rearview mirror. "Drink up!" I call back to Mila.

She jams the straw into her mouth and sucks hard before yanking it back out. "Yuck! It's OJ. I hate OJ!"

"Mommy probably got mixed up. But we wouldn't want to waste it, would we?"

Mila's shoulders slump, a worried pucker forming on her forehead. "No. Mommy doesn't have much money anymore."

"That's right!" I say, beaming at her. "What a good girl you are for being so caring and kind!"

She sighs dramatically, sucking noisily as though to

drive home the sacrifice she's making—for which I'm truly grateful.

Minutes later, she's out cold, her head tilting to one side at an awkward angle. I really should stop and lay her down on the seat, so she doesn't get a crick in her neck. *Yeah, right!* But I do need to hide her. As soon as we're out of town, I'll find somewhere inconspicuous to pull over. There's bound to be a BOLO alert out for me by now, but I've already changed out my license plates so that should buy me enough time to get across the border. With a little persuasion, Cash will join me. He won't want to be parted from his daughter, and this is the only way we can all be together. We can finally start over somewhere new, like I've been telling him all along. With Anya out of the way, there will be no one to contest custody, the abduction charges will be dropped, and we can be a family. As a bonus, I'll never have to set eyes on Eleanor again. Nothing could persuade her to visit Mexico. Good riddance!

I pull off the freeway at a rest stop and park away from the other vehicles clustered around the bathrooms and vending machines. I sit for a few minutes, observing cars come and go, making sure no one's paying me any attention, before reaching back and unbuckling Mila. I lay her down on the seat and throw a blanket over her. I give it another minute or two, before climbing out and retrieving an over-sized duffle bag from the trunk of my car. Sliding into the back seat next to Mila, I carefully maneuver her limp frame inside, still swathed in the blanket. I leave the zipper partway open to make sure she has plenty of air, even though the canvas looks thin enough to breathe through. Out of an abundance of caution, I take out my pocketknife and make several slits in the fabric. She's no good to me dead.

When I'm satisfied with the set up, I exit the car and carry the bag around to the trunk. *Sorry, kid. It's only 'til we cross the border.* I slam the trunk closed and stroll nonchalantly to the driver's door. I'm about to climb back into my seat when a familiar voice startles me. "Going somewhere?"

I freeze, eyes widening as my head jerks toward Wade. "What are you doing here?" I hiss.

His lips curl into a sneer. "Funny, I was going to ask you the same thing."

"I hired you to follow Cash, not me," I say, casting a glance over my shoulder to make sure we're out of earshot of any passersby.

Wade chuckles in an unpleasant kind of way. "You hired me for a lot of things. I'm the one who found you that punk graffiti kid to play your stupid pranks, and I'm the one who torched Eleanor's place when he chickened out. Or have you forgotten everything I did for you?"

"You got your money. What do you want, Wade?"

He takes a step closer and lowers his voice. "Compensation. You know what for."

"I have no idea what you're talking about."

"Don't play games with me. You killed my old lady and tried to pin it on me."

56

LEXI

I narrow my eyes at Wade. "I had nothing to do with your mother's fall."

He stuffs his hands into his pockets. "Not that I'm complaining. You did me a favor. The house is mine now, so I can afford to be reasonable. Let's say ... one hundred thousand dollars."

I throw back my head and laugh. "Are you seriously trying to blackmail me? I hate to break it to you, Wade, but you have nothing to hold over my head. It's preposterous to think I did anything to your mother. You're as deeply embroiled in this as I am. If you try and pull a fast one, you're going down with me."

A cunning smile creeps over his lips. "I don't think so. Your husband came to see me the other night. He said if I can help nail the case against you, I'll get full immunity." He nods, as if agreeing with himself. "The thing is, I don't like wheeling and dealing with cops any more than you do. So I figure if we can work out our own deal with terms satisfactory to both parties, that would be the way to go." He shrugs, hands still plunged deep into his pockets. "It's your call—your life to live, as they say."

I breathe slowly in and out through my nostrils. "Fine. Get in the car. You can drive us to the bank. I'll give you your money and then I don't want to see you ever again—understood?"

Wade grins, his discolored teeth on full display as he yanks open the driver's door. I climb in after him, wrinkling my nose at the body odor now permeating my car. I crack my window and tell him to do the same.

"You're gonna have to bring me back here after you get me my money," he says, jerking his head in the direction of Helen's beat-up Oldsmobile.

I'm pretty sure Wade doesn't have a valid driver's license but that's the least of my concerns right now. I need to figure out how to get rid of him before I reach the border. It shouldn't be too challenging—he's dumb enough to think I can walk into a bank and withdraw one hundred thousand dollars at the drop of a hat, even if I had that kind of money to begin with.

"Where were you heading? Leaving him, are you?" Wade asks, one arm dangling out the window.

"Of course not. We're moving out of the area to get away from Jess and all her nonsense—Eleanor too. Cash will be joining me."

"Except it wasn't all her nonsense, was it? You were framing her all along." He turns his head and eyes me curiously. "Where is she anyway?"

"No one knows."

"They found her car. The cops reckon she bled out in it." He shakes his head. "She was a looker, I'll give Cash that. But he should have known he'd get busted, stringing two women along."

It feels as if there are bombs going off inside my head. How does he know what the cops are saying? I fight the urge to reach for Wade and smash his face against the window. *It won't benefit you, Lexi*, I tell myself. *He'll crash and then the police will arrive on the scene. You don't want that, remember?*

"Hey! You listening to me, or what?" Wade yells, startling me out of my catatonic state. "How much longer to the bank?"

I think of a number. "Fifteen minutes. But I need to gas up first. I have a long trip ahead of me. Get off at the next exit."

Minutes later, Wade pulls into a gas station and jerks to a stop at the pump.

"Easy!" I admonish him. I can't risk Mila getting injured. "When's the last time you drove a car?"

He shrugs. "Last time the old lady let me have the keys." He winks at me. "That won't be a problem anymore, thanks to you."

I shudder as I climb out. Leaving the nozzle in the fuel tank, I walk into the store to grab some snacks, still trying to finalize my plan to get rid of Wade. As I exit the front door, I catch sight of him closing the trunk of the car. My stomach drops. What was he doing in there? Did he open the bag? Heart racing, I bolt across to the car and climb in.

Wade stares straight ahead, both hands gripping the wheel like he's superglued to it. When he turns to me, there's a frenzied look in his eyes. I'm not sure if he's high, or terrified, or both.

"There's ... a kid ... in the bag. Is that Cash's kid? What have you done?"

57

CASH

I jump up from my chair in the surgery waiting area as soon as Price walks back in. "Any updates?"

"Not yet. We have a BOLO out, and officers stopping traffic—"

"Stopping traffic?" I clench my fists in front of me, fighting the urge to punch something or someone. "Is this some kind of joke? My six-year-old daughter's missing and all you're doing is stopping traffic. Lexi could be close to the border by now."

Price raises his hands in an effort to placate me. "We've alerted border security. They're going to be watching for a woman and a child. They have her description, car make, model, color, license plate. She's not going to be able to cross into Mexico without being detained."

I take a step toward him. "You can't guarantee that. You totally underestimated her—we all did." I swallow back the fear surging up my throat as Lexi's words come back to haunt me: *you never really know what someone's capable of until they're pushed to their limits.* At the time, I thought she was talking about Anya. Looking back, I can see what a fool

I was. Do I believe she would harm Mila? Yes! A resounding yes. If she has no use for her anymore, she'll dispose of her. At all costs, I have to make sure that doesn't happen.

Eleanor arrives on the scene just as Price is getting ready to make his exit. "I got here as quickly as I could. Traffic is horrendous," she announces. "Is Anya out of surgery yet?"

I shake my head, not trusting myself to speak. I'm filled with emotion at the sight of her. Despite her catty, condescending ways, I know she loves me fiercely, and she was right about Lexi. She smelled a rat from the outset. If only I'd listened to her.

"Where's Mila? Did Lexi take her to the cafeteria?" my mother asks, her gaze sweeping down the hall in search of her only grandchild.

I nod to Price. "Go do what you need to do to find her. I'll fill my mother in."

He takes off down the corridor, radio crackling.

My mother turns to me. "What's he doing here? Are they any closer to finding Jess?"

"Sit down, Mom," I say, grabbing her by the hand and pulling her gently into a seat. "I wasn't talking about Jess. I was talking about Mila. Lexi's taken her."

My mother tilts her spindly brows inward. "Taken her where?"

"Taken her, as in abducted her. The police think she did something to Jess too. She's been pretending to be Jess all along."

Mom stares at me, motionless, like I've put her under a spell. I know exactly what she's experiencing as her brain struggles to piece it together, the cogs slowly turning until the lock clicks open and there it is—staring you in the face, what you should have realized all along. Kind, sweet, naive, selfless Lexi is actually a psychopathic arsonist and murderer.

"The police are looking for her and Mila right now."

She shakes her head. "I'm so sorry, son," she says at length, her tone unusually subdued.

"It's not your fault. I'm sorry for accusing you of things you didn't do."

"I meant I'm sorry ... about Jess. Maybe if I had been more welcoming, she might not have made the decision to leave you."

I pass a hand over my eyes, discreetly wiping my damp lashes. "That's on me. I'm the one who forced her to choose between me or her PhD. To this day, I don't know why I was so stubborn. She could have had both. I could have waited a couple more years to start our family. Now, I'll never have the chance."

Mom is silent for a moment, as if pondering something. "Lexi was never really pregnant, was she? I was never going to have another grandchild."

I raise my brows. "No, she wasn't. How did you know?"

She twists her hands in her lap. "Woman's intuition. I always thought it was odd she never put on an ounce."

My phone starts buzzing and I glance at it absently. *Unknown number.* My skin prickles. It could be the police, but then again it could be her. "I have to take this call," I say, striding over to the door. "Will you stay here and wait for news of Anya?"

She nods. "Of course. Let me know the minute you hear Mila's safe."

I press the phone to my ear as I walk briskly down the corridor in the direction of the hospital exit. "Hello?"

There's an elongated moment of silence before I hear

Lexi's voice. "Meet me in Ensenada tonight. I'll text you an address once you get here."

"Lexi! Wait! Let me talk to Mila!"

"She's sleeping right now. You are going to come, aren't you, Cash? This is our chance to start over like we talked about. Free of Jess and Eleanor and Anya. No more ghosts from the past. Just you, me, and Mila. This is what we *both* want, Cash." Her voice is insistent, maniacal almost, begging for validation. I clutch the phone, terrified of saying the wrong thing. The last thing I want is for her to hang up on me. I'm desperate to know Mila's safe.

"Of course it is," I assure her, hurrying out through the automatic doors. "You know how much I've always wanted a family."

"And children of our own," Lexi adds. "We can try again."

I hesitate for a moment, my heart clattering at breakneck speed. This is the wrong time to call her out on her lies. She might hurt Mila in a fit of jealous rage. "Can you wake Mila up for just a minute so I can say a quick *hi* to her."

"You'll see her tonight," Lexi fires back, her tone reverting to one of barely repressed anger. I swallow the knot in my throat. She's a pot of wrath about to boil over at any second, and whoever's in her path is going to get scalded.

"Sure, that's fine," I soothe. "I'm walking to my car as we speak. Are you at a hotel?"

"Don't concern yourself about my whereabouts. I said I'll text you the address when you get here. I'll handle everything."

I'm about to respond when I hear a muffled male voice in the background. I frown, listening intently, but I can't make out the exchange. Lexi must have covered the speaker.

I run a hand over the back of my neck. Is she with someone else? Or talking to someone in passing? I can't decide if this is a good thing or a bad thing. She's unlikely to harm Mila if there's someone else there, but I don't like the idea of a strange male hanging around my daughter either. My head pounds as I unlock my car and jump in. I put my phone on speaker and turn on the ignition. The gas gauge is at three-quarters of a tank. It should be enough to get me there without having to make a stop.

As I wheel out of the parking lot, Lexi comes back on the line. "Are you driving yet?"

"Yes. I just left the hospital."

There's a loaded pause before she asks, "Is everything okay?"

I try to keep my tone measured as I respond, playing along with her insanity. "Anya took a nasty fall down the stairs. She's in surgery. I don't know if she's going to make it."

"I'm not surprised. She drinks too much," Lexi says abruptly. "It's best for Mila that she'll be with us from now on."

I grit my teeth as I force the words out. "Yeah, you're right."

"I'm going to hang up now so you can concentrate on getting here safely. You have until 9:00 P.M."

I glance at my watch. It's shortly after five, which gives me plenty of time to cross the border and make it to Ensenada, and plenty of time for Price to contact the Mexican authorities and coordinate Lexi's arrest.

"Oh, and Cash," Lexi says breezily. "Don't even think about alerting the police. You do want your daughter to wake up from her nap, don't you?"

58

LEXI

I pull out a KitKat and offer it to Wade.

"It's her—Mila—isn't it?" He swats the candy bar away, his eyes bulging. "You're sick, you know that? I'm calling the cops."

He reaches for the car door handle but freezes when he feels the gun pressing into his back.

"Turn around and start the engine, Wade. Nothing's going to happen to the kid. You're misunderstanding what's happening here. Jess tried to kill Mila's mother today. Cash asked me to take Mila to safety before Jess gets to her too. Now, drive!"

Wade's eyes twitch suspiciously. "So why's she in the bag?"

I sigh. "Isn't it obvious? Cash was afraid Jess would follow me if she saw Mila in the car."

"You drugged her," Wade says accusingly.

"It's only Benadryl, just enough to let her sleep through the trip. Don't worry, she was excited to hide in the bag when Cash told her it was a game."

"Why'd you put her in the trunk?" Wade asks, stubbornly refusing to start the car.

I take the safety off the gun and jab it at him again. "Shut up and drive!"

He sniffs defiantly. "Not until you take the kid out of the trunk. She could roll around in there and hurt herself. Jess won't be able to see her if she's in the bag on the back seat, so what's the difference?"

I grimace. "Fine! Get her out, but don't try anything stupid. Make one wrong move and your dream of getting any more money out of me is over."

Wade wipes his sleeve across his nose and clambers out of the car. I watch him like a hawk as he walks around to the back and opens the trunk. I'm half afraid he'll try to run off with the bag, but I guess he really does think he's going to get his money because he opens the back door and slides the bag onto the seat. He throws a wary glance around, then slams the door shut on Mila. I let out a sigh of relief, but before he can climb back into the car, I glimpse a flash of brown fur and Wade suddenly slams to the ground. He screams and gyrates on the asphalt as an enormous German Shepherd chows down on his arm. I watch in horror as a man runs up pointing a gun at Wade.

"Break!" he yells to the dog, which instantly releases its grip on Wade's arm. The man flashes a badge at him. "Officer Bryant, Narcotics. Got any drugs on you, sir?"

I breathe slowly in and out. An undercover police officer. What are the odds? As unobtrusively as possible, I place my gun on the floor by my feet.

Wade sits up, clutching his arm and moaning.

Officer Bryant glances inside the car. "I'm gonna need you to step out of the car too, ma'am."

I nudge my gun under the seat with my foot, and climb out, hands raised. "What's this about, Officer?"

"My dog detected drugs on your partner here."

I raise my brows in a gesture of shock. "There must be some kind of misunderstanding."

Ignoring me, Bryant jerks his chin at Wade, "On your feet. What's your name, sir?"

"Wade Powers." He struggles to stand, muttering and swearing.

Bryant swiftly pats him down, pulling a baggie from Wade's coat pocket. He sniffs it, then whips out a pair of handcuffs. "That's at least five ounces. Got a record, have you, Wade?"

He scowls back at him, as Officer Bryant cuffs him and directs him to sit down on the curb.

"Is this your car?"

"It's mine," I interrupt. "I don't do drugs. I had no idea my friend had any on him, Officer."

Bryant gives a curt nod. "You don't mind if I let Shadow take a quick sniff around."

I swallow hard. "Um ..."

Without waiting for a response, he walks Shadow slowly around the car, taking extra time at the trunk. My heart pounds erratically the entire time but, to my relief, Shadow doesn't seem remotely interested.

"What's in the duffle bag?" Bryant asks, peering through the window into the back seat.

"Just clothing," I answer glibly.

"Going somewhere?"

Wade's eyes bore into me. I can sense him weighing his decision to rat me out. I knew he'd be a liability. I should have gotten rid of him the minute I set eyes on him.

"We're just taking a quick trip south of the border," I say.

Bryant hefts a brow. "Mexico?"

I nod, beaming. "I have a couple of days off."

Wade looks straight at me, his lips twisting into a spiteful grin. "There's a kid in the bag, Officer."

59

LEXI

P rice ambles into the room and takes a seat, arranging his pudgy hands on the desk in front of him. I stare at them, repulsed by the doughy mountain of flesh. It seems I underestimated him. His brain operates at a speed deceptively faster than his body moves. My head pounds as I backtrack through his maneuvering over the last few days. He played a brilliant hand, making me believe he was investigating my husband. My adamant denials that Cash was involved in any way only served to strengthen his suspicion that I knew more than I was leading him to believe. It remains to be seen how much he really knows.

He flicks open the folder in front of him, and starts recording, noting the time and names of those present.

I watch as he thumbs through several pages before landing on the one he's looking for. "You understand you've been arrested on charges of kidnapping a minor and child endangerment?"

I shrug. "It was a simple misunderstanding. I was trying

to keep Mila safe from Jess. She had just attacked her mother. I told Cash all this already."

Price taps his pen methodically on his notebook.

I feel like someone's jamming a poker in my eye. He thinks he knows how to push me to my breaking point—he doesn't. I don't have one.

"Speaking of Anya, she came through her surgery and is making a remarkable recovery." Price makes his distinctive hacking sound at the back of his throat. "She's been telling me about her ... fall. She also mentioned you two had coffee together in the mall that morning. Cash gave me the impression you didn't get along. What was your meeting about?"

The leaden weight in the pit of my stomach grows ever more uncomfortable. I was counting on Anya not pulling through. I can't believe Eleanor came back early and interrupted me before I could finish the job. I was forced to make a speedy exit and never got to confirm that Anya actually broke her neck in the fall.

"Anya wanted to talk to me about what we'd discovered on Eleanor's computer. I still think she was helping Eleanor all along. Cash suspects she broke into our house and stole the gun."

"Why would she do that?"

"Her marriage to Anton had ended in an ugly divorce, and she had nowhere to live. Eleanor offered her a place to stay but it came with strings attached—helping her and Jess get rid of me. She went along with it, at first, but I think she felt guilty." I lean forward to make sure I have Price's full attention. "She was very depressed about it all. Maybe she tried to take her own life."

Price's nose twitches. "Did she ever admit to any of the harassment?"

I shrug. "Not in so many words. But she told me Eleanor

made her keep receipts for everything. Have you checked her phone? There could be a paper trail."

Price jots something down on his notepad and underlines it. "I'll look into it." He knots his brows together. "What I'd like to talk to you about right now is Jessica Spicer's disappearance."

I give an exaggerated sigh. "I have no idea where she is, but I can tell you this—Cash and I hope we never see or hear of her again."

"The problem I'm having is that your story of being harassed has holes in it."

I cock a skeptical brow. "What are you referring to? If it's dates, I can go back over them, if you like. Cash and I kept a meticulous log."

Price gives a thoughtful nod before glancing down at his notes again. "Oddly enough, the harassing messages all came from VPN's associated with your server. In fact, we found the exact photos in your iCloud account that Jess supposedly sent to Cash to prove it was her texting him— one of a blonde woman lying bound and gagged, another of Jess in Maui, the gun, and several other items including Jess's driver's license."

I press my lips into a tight line. *Careless, Lexi! Very careless.* I thought I'd deleted everything. I forgot about the random file folder I'd titled *medical records*.

"I think you know a lot more about Jessica Spicer's disappearance than you're letting on," Price says.

"I have no idea where those photos came from, but I suspect she planted them on my computer when she broke into my house."

Price stares at me, an icy calm in his eyes. "She didn't plant your hair in her blood."

My tongue feels like it's glued to the roof of my mouth.

"That's right," he goes on, a sneer curling his fat lips. "Your hair, not your husband's, was mixed with her blood. That puts you at the scene of the crime."

My hands curl into fists beneath the table. "I want a lawyer."

"I bet you do." Price leans back in his chair and begins tapping his pen again. *Rat-a-tat-tat. Rat-a-tat-tat.* I stare at it, willing it to stop, but it continues unabated.

Rat-a-tat-tat. Rat-a-tat-tat. Rat-a-tat-tat. Rat-a-tat-tat.

And just like that my brain explodes. I leap out of my chair and snatch the pen from his hand, stabbing it into his neck with all the momentum my rage grants me in the moment.

Maybe I didn't finish the job with Anya, but I won't make that mistake twice.

60

CASH

The relief I feel as I hold Mila in my arms again is incalculable. I rub my hand over her soft curls, blinking back tears when I think about how close I came to losing her. Lexi was only forty minutes from the border when she was apprehended. It's beyond shocking to think I have Wade to thank for that—Wade and a particularly diligent K-9 called Shadow. That's one of the great things about dogs: they don't even know when they're heroes.

"Can I go play in my room now, Daddy?" Mila asks, wriggling free of my grip.

"Sure thing. I'll let you know when Nana gets here." I smile to myself as I watch her bolt from the room. She's a good reminder of everything I still have to live for, despite my second marriage imploding in the worst way possible.

Lexi is being held without bail after attacking Price at the station. Turns out, she missed his carotid artery, and it ended up being a superficial wound from which he'll make a full recovery. I can hardly get my head around the fact that it took three officers to pull her off him and restrain her. All this time, I thought of my wife—soon-to-be ex-wife—as a fragile and sensitive soul. But it was only a mask to give her the appearance of normalcy, a construct to confuse her prey. She sized me up from the beginning, recognized that I was vulnerable, and pretended to give me what I desired most— a happy family—so she could control me. For whatever reason, she became obsessed with becoming my soulmate, as if that was something she could cultivate. It's not. It's a gift from God that none of us deserve and few of us discover— instantly recognizable but rarely replicable.

"Cash, I'm here!" Mom calls out as she comes through the front door. She's agreed to watch Mila while I go to the prison to visit Lexi. I'm not going out of any concern for her, it's only for closure, to let her know in person that I'm filing for divorce and ask how she would like me to dispose of her belongings. The sooner they're out of my house, the better.

"Thanks for doing this," I say, giving my mother a concili-atory hug—the first I've given her since I banned her from my house. She may be catty, petty, and silly, and a host of other five-letter words, but I can't discount the fact that she stuck by me when my father walked out. She's the only mother I'll ever have, and I'm grateful I didn't lose her during Lexi's psychopathic rampage.

"How's Anya doing?" I ask.

Mom sets down her purse with a sigh. "Black and blue, but thankful to be alive. She apologized to me for every awful thing she's ever said about me, and actually thanked me for letting her and Mila move in. I think this brush with death has given her a whole new outlook on life."

"It will do that to you," I say.

Mom takes off her coat and hangs it up. "She found out this morning her phone had been tampered with. Appar-ently, Lexi asked Price if he'd checked Anya's phone for any evidence that she was conspiring with me. Anya found some photos of receipts for accelerant and bleach. Lexi must have accessed her phone and uploaded them at some point."

"It doesn't surprise me," I say, reaching for my keys. "Thanks again for watching Mila. I'll be back before dinner."

"Don't be late. I'm making your favorite—pasta with shrimp and sun-dried tomatoes."

"Thanks Mom. You're the best."

She gives a tight nod. "Not always. I may have added fuel to the fire a time or two. I have to confess I deliberately made my chicken casserole for Lexi after she told you she couldn't stand it. Upon reflection, it was the wrong thing to do."

I snort out a laugh. "In the grand scheme of things, it rates as a low-level crime, so you're forgiven."

My phone starts ringing and I groan. It's been ringing off the hook since the news broke—Tom, all the guys, work colleagues, extended family. For the most part, I'm letting the calls go to voicemail. I reluctantly pull my phone out of my pocket and glance at the screen.

"Officer Price," I say, taking the call. "How are you feeling?"

"Fine. It was just a puncture wound." He chuckles. "I knew those rolls of fat would come in useful one day." He clears his throat, and I close my eyes in preparation for bad news. "Cash, I wanted to tell you before you hear it on the news—camera crews are already on-site."

My blood runs cold. I lock eyes with my mother, seeking support from the only parent I ever knew. "O-kay," I say, my voice suddenly unsteady.

"We found human remains near where Jess's car was discovered."

"Is it ... her?"

There's a long pause before Price responds. "We'll have to wait for DNA tests to confirm. The body was doused in accelerant and burned in a makeshift campfire."

I heave a breath in and out, a barrage of images flashing through my mind; snorkeling with Jess in Maui—watching the joy breaking out on her sunlit face as a turtle swam by, feeding the ducks at the park as we did our best to imitate their moves, making out on our favorite bench while shooing away the seagulls trying to snatch up our chips, running hand-in-hand through the rain as we laughed hysterically at the odd, squelching sounds our shoes made, talking long into the night about our hopes and dreams for our lives, our children's lives, and the world in general. I let out a guttural sob. My soulmate is lost to me forever. Why couldn't I have swallowed my pride and told her I couldn't live without her, no matter her terms? Why couldn't I have told Lexi I wasn't in love with her, and never would be. How did I turn out to be such a coward?

Price ends the call, and my mother lays a hand on my arm. "Are you sure you still want to go to the prison? You can do it another day."

I give a grim shake of my head. "There's no day I'd rather do it. I need to look her in the eye and tell her to her face what she's done to me."

61

CASH

My chest feels so tight, even breathing hurts as I pass through several layers of security at the California Institution for Women. Maybe this wasn't the best idea after all. I could have handled everything through lawyers, avoided another face-to-face confrontation with the woman who took so much from me. It's only now when it's been lost to me forever that I realize just how valuable it was.

"Hey! Your stuff," a bored-looking prison guard says, gesturing with his chin to my car keys and the legal envelope lying on the conveyer belt.

I snap myself out of my stupor and follow the rest of the group to the visiting room where I find an empty table and slump down in a plastic chair to wait. The minutes tick by as, one by one, the other tables fill up with inmates and visitors. It's evident from body language and gestures that some of the conversations are tense. I have no idea how Lexi will react to seeing me here. She's still in denial about everything, even as the evidence against her continues to mount. Maybe she'll fly at me and try to claw my eyes out. I can't imagine any of the other visitors are up against anything close to what I'm dealing with.

I flinch when a flash of orange comes into view. The chair opposite me scrapes over the floor as Lexi slumps into it. My mouth gapes open at her altered state. Her hair looks as if she hasn't combed it since her arrest. Her face is gaunt, her prison garb hanging askew from her scrawny frame.

"Do you ... want something from the vending machine?" I ask. I don't know why I make the offer—just following the visitors' playbook, I guess.

"I'd kill for a hazelnut latte," she says with a wink designed to be seductive, but which makes me shudder and look away.

"How come you haven't been answering your phone? I've been calling you," she says, locking an all-too-familiar pitiful gaze on me. I used to think it signaled fragility, like a flower needing protection from the raging elements. Now, I see it for what it is—a calculated attempt to cloak the darkness within. When I look at her now, I can see straight through to the empty pit where her soul should be.

I open the envelope I brought and put the paperwork from my lawyer on the table between us. "I'm filing for divorce. Let me know what you want me to do with your belongings. I can have them packed up and delivered wherever you want."

She gives an uneasy laugh. "This isn't what you want. You want a family with me, remember?"

"I thought you were someone else. It's the end of the road for us."

"It's never the end. We can fight these charges together." She lowers her voice and leans toward me. "I was only trying to protect Mila from Jess."

I catch the eye of the officer surveying the room from his

booth in the corner, like a hawk ready to swoop in at a moment's notice.

I lean back in my chair, putting as much distance between myself and Lexi as possible. "You're never getting out of prison," I say. "You're going to be tried for murder, as well as kidnapping and a host of other charges."

"But you and I know the truth," she whines. "You have to help me. You're my husband."

"Not for much longer. Marrying you was the worst mistake I ever made."

Her face darkens. "You said you wanted to start a family. You wanted me to give you what Jess wouldn't give you. She was too selfish."

"Don't you dare say her name." I grind out the words, barely able to keep myself from punching the smug grin off her face. "I know what you did to her."

Lexi rolls her eyes. "Not this again. You know I don't have the stomach for murder. I'm sorry she met such a grisly fate, but that's what happens when you run from the law and try and hide out in some desolate place. Some hunter probably shot her by accident and panicked, then tried to cover up his mistake. Or maybe it was some drugged-up homeless schmuck. You can't be too careful nowadays."

I shake my head in disbelief. "Is that your best defense? You're a sick individual, Lexi, and you're beyond help if you can't even acknowledge what you've done, let alone be remorseful for it."

"Time's up!" The guard calls out from across the room.

I stand, immensely relieved the visit has come to an end. I will walk out of here and never return. I will never have to hear her grating voice in my ear again.

Lexi gets to her feet slowly, her chair scraping the floor as she scoots it back. "Think about what I said. You and I belong together." She pulls back her lips and whispers, "The hunter and the prey."

I look at her for what I hope will be the last time outside of the trial. "I just want to know why. Why did you do it?"

She shrugs. "If you want something in life, you have to reach for it with both hands. I wanted what she had—your heart."

A peculiar smile spreads over her face. "Don't you know, Cash, that the heart is the prize of every hunter."

A QUICK FAVOR

Dear Reader,

I hope you enjoyed reading *All But Safe* as much as I enjoyed writing it. Thank you for taking the time to check out my books and I would appreciate it from the bottom of my heart if you would leave a review on Amazon or Goodreads as it makes a HUGE difference in helping new readers find the series. Thank you!

To be the first to hear about my upcoming book releases, sales, and fun giveaways, join my newsletter at

**https://normahinkens.-
com/newsletter**

and follow me on Twitter, Instagram and Facebook. Feel free to email me at norma@normahinkens.com with any feedback or comments. I LOVE hearing from readers. YOU are the reason I keep writing!

All my best,
Norma

WHAT YOU WISH FOR

Check out **What You Wish For,** *the second book in the* **Wicked Ways Collection.**

Am I scaring you yet?

Already a father to a four-year-old daughter with his ex-wife, Cash makes a spur-of-the-moment decision to marry his girlfriend of five months, Lexi, when she unexpectedly falls pregnant.

Three weeks later, still in the throes of newlywed bliss, Lexi is brutally attacked in an underground parking garage, resulting in the tragic loss of their baby.

Freshly discharged from the hospital, she returns home to find her car spray-painted with a horrifying message from someone threatening to finish the job: *next time the knife goes through your heart.*

It's the beginning of a nightmarish chain of events that won't end well. As a dangerous net of harassment tightens, Lexi begins to question everyone around her, including her new husband.

Can she unravel the chilling web of lies her life has become before it's too late?

- A high-octane thriller with a spellbinding cast of characters and a breathtaking twist! -

WHAT TO READ NEXT

Ready for another thrilling read with shocking twists and a
mind-blowing murder plot?

Explore my entire lineup of thrillers on Amazon or at
https://normahinkens.com/thrillers

Do you enjoy reading across genres? I also write young
adult science fiction and fantasy thrillers. You can find out
more about those titles at
https://normahinkens.com/YAbooks

BIOGRAPHY

NYT and USA Today bestselling author N. L. Hinkens writes twisty psychological suspense thrillers with unexpected endings. She's a travel junkie, coffee hound, and idea wrangler, in no particular order. She grew up in Ireland—land of legends and storytelling—and now resides in the US. Her work has won the Grand Prize Next Generation Indie Book Award for fiction, as well as numerous other awards. Check out her newsletter for hot new releases, stellar giveaways, exclusive content, behind the scenes and more.

https://normahinkens.com/newsletter

Follow her on Facebook for funnies, giveaways, cool stuff & more!

https://normahinkens.com/Facebook

BOOKS BY N. L. HINKENS

SHOP THE ENTIRE CATALOG HERE

https://normahinkens.com/thrillers

VILLAINOUS VACATIONS COLLECTION

- The Cabin Below
- You Will Never Leave
- Her Last Steps

DOMESTIC DECEPTIONS COLLECTION

- Never Tell Them
- I Know What You Did
- The Other Woman

PAYBACK PASTS COLLECTION

- The Class Reunion
- The Lies She Told
- Right Behind You

TREACHEROUS TRIPS COLLECTION

- Wrong Exit
- The Invitation
- While She Slept

WICKED WAYS COLLECTION

- All But Safe
- What You Wish For

NOVELLAS

- The Silent Surrogate

BOOKS BY NORMA HINKENS

I also write young adult science fiction and fantasy thrillers under Norma Hinkens.

https://normahinkens.com/YAbooks

THE UNDERGROUNDERS SERIES
POST-APOCALYPTIC

- Immurement
- Embattlement
- Judgement

THE EXPULSION PROJECT
SCIENCE FICTION

- Girl of Fire
- Girl of Stone
- Girl of Blood

THE KEEPERS CHRONICLES
EPIC FANTASY

- Opal of Light
- Onyx of Darkness
- Opus of Doom

FOLLOW NORMA

FOLLOW NORMA:

Sign up for her newsletter:
https://normahinkens.com/newsletter
Website:
https://normahinkens.com/
Facebook:
https://normahinkens.com/Facebook
Twitter
https://normahinkens.com/Twitter
Instagram
https://normahinkens.com/Instagram
Pinterest:
https://normahinkens.com/Pinterest

Printed in the USA
CPSIA information can be obtained
at www.ICGtesting.com
LVHW090327121223
766265LV00041B/437